The Selected Works

Mahasweta Devi (b. 1926) is one of our fore... sonalities, a prolific and best-selling author in Bengali of short fiction and novels; a deeply political social activist who has been working with and for tribals and marginalized communities like the landless labourers of eastern India for years; the editor of a quarterly, *Bortika*, in which the tribals and marginalized peoples themselves document grassroot-level issues and trends; and a socio-political commentator whose articles have appeared regularly in the *Economic and Political Weekly*, *Frontier* and other journals.

Mahasweta Devi has made important contributions to literary and cultural studies in this country. Her empirical research into oral history as it lives in the cultures and memories of tribal communities was a first of its kind. Her powerful, haunting tales of exploitation and struggle have been seen as rich sites of feminist discourse by leading scholars. Her innovative use of language has expanded the conventional borders of Bengali literary expression. Standing as she does at the intersection of vital contemporary questions of politics, gender and class, she is a significant figure in the field of socially committed literature.

Recognizing this, we have conceived a publishing programme which encompasses a representational look at the complete Mahasweta: her novels, her short fiction, her children's stories, her plays, her activist prose writings. The series is an attempt to introduce her impressive body of work to a readership beyond Bengal; it is also an overdue recognition of the importance of her contribution to the literary and cultural history of our country.

Mother of 1084
Translated by Samik Bandyopadhyay

Breast Stories
Translated by
Gayatri Chakravorty Spivak

Five Plays
Translated by Samik Bandyopadhyay

Rudali: From Fiction to Performance
Translated by Anjum Katyal

Dust on the Road:
The Activist Writings of Mahasweta Devi
Translated by Maitreya Ghatak

Bitter Soil
Translated by Ipsita Chanda

Our Non-Veg Cow and Other Stories
Translated by Paramita Banerjee

The Armenian Champa Tree
Translated by Nirmal Kanti
Bhattacharjee

Old Women
Translated by
Gayatri Chakravorty Spivak

Titu Mir
Translated by Rimi B. Chatterjee

The Queen of Jhansi
Translated by Mandira
and Sagaree Sengupta

Till Death Do Us Part
Translated by Vikram Iyengar

The Book of the Hunter
Translated by Mandira
and Sagaree Sengupta

Chotti Munda and His Arrow
Translated by
Gayatri Chakravorty Spivak

The Glory of Sree Sree Ganesh
Translated by Ipsita Chanda

Dewana, Khoimala
and the Holy Banyan Tree
Translated by Pinaki Bhattacharya

Romtha
Translated by Pinaki Bhattacharya

In the Name of the Mother
Translated by Radha Chakravarty

Wrong Number and Other Stories
Translated by Subhransu Maitra

After Kurukshetra
Translated by Anjum Katyal

Bait.
Translated by Sumanta Banerjee

Bedanabala. Her Life. Her Times.
Translated by Sunandini Banerjee

OUTCAST

FOUR STORIES

MAHASWETA DEVI

Translated by
SARMISTHA DUTTA GUPTA

Seagull Books

LONDON NEW YORK CALCUTTA

First Printing 2002
Second Printing 2007
Third Printing 2011
Fourth Printing 2015

'Chinta' was published in *Ki Boshontey Ki Shorotey*, 1959; 'Dhouli' in *Nairitey Megh*, 1979; 'Shanichari' and 'Rajabashar Rupkatha' in *Eenter Porey Eent*, 1982.

ISBN 978 81 7046 189 0

Published by Naveen Kishore, on behalf of Seagull Books Private Limited, 31A S. P. Mukherjee Road, Calcutta 700 025

Printed and bound by Hyam Enterprises, Calcutta

CONTENTS

Translator's Note

DHOULI, SHANICHARI, JOSMINA AND CHINTA—grouping these four women in a single volume was a difficult decision. Some may find it a lugubrious collection, given the fact that all these women are victims of the most severe kinds of exploitation in Indian society—the exploitation of women, to many, is a cliché. Should it form the basis of a selection? So before I finally selected these stories, I went through a mental tussle. Should I include a more cheerful story, perhaps one where the woman was not just a victim, one that ended on a note of hope? After much thought, I decided that Dhouli, Shanichari, Josmina and Chinta could be comfortable only in each others' company. That it was facile to search for something far removed from reality. And also that Dhouli, Shanichari, Josmina and Chinta are not just victims, each subtly forcing her community to rethink societal norms. Hence the grouping of these stories in a single collection.

When I began translating 'Chinta', it took me a few days to go beyond the first two sentences. Every time I read the lines, it hit me somewhere in my gut. I was too close to the story, its idiom and milieu. My middle-class complacency was rudely shaken each time I went through it. I had wanted to translate this story ever since I first read it, years ago. I had thought that it wouldn't be all that difficult, given the fact that 'Chinta' was set in Kolkata's Ballygunge, that my active pool of words would come in handy. But 'Chinta' completely overturned these notions.

I have tried to translate the stories in a way that the meaning of most Indian words italicized in the text becomes clear through their context. At times, I have also chosen to reject English equivalents of Indian words easily found in dictionaries. For example, I have retained mela and not translated it into 'fair' or 'village fair'. Similarly, I have used *gur* and not 'molasses' and *khaini* instead of 'chewing tobacco'. I do not consider it sacrosanct to always conform to an accepted register of Indian English, as it were, because I believe every translator should have the freedom to define his/her own terms of writing.

For negotiating the different registers of Mahasweta's Bangla I have, at times, found punctuation to be one of the most effective tools. I tried this out in 'Shanichari' where there are at least half a dozen registers. Shanichari and her grandmother, the Adivasi Raksha Morcha, the Bihar Military Police, the press, the politicians, and the brick kiln owners all speak in distinctly individual voices. Whereas in the original their voices flow through long paragraphs, in the translation I deliberately signposted these as a series of individual lines within quotes and occasionally left the sentences incomplete, using ellipses frequently. The visual impact of these lines, I thought, would help the reader gauge to some extent what couldn't be conveyed through words.

The author occasionally uses English words in her Bengali prose. These have been spelt phonetically, in an attempt to mark them out from Bangla, and simultaneously indicate that they are not identical with the conventional English usage. Moreover, the speakers in the text are not a monolithic group; they would have pronounced these words variously. Thus, the word 'leader' is spelt *leedar*, 'partner' as *paatnar*. I am grateful to Anjum Katyal for this suggestion.

Working closely with the author has been a tremendous help in ensuring that there are no misreadings. Mahasweta's prose contains many words which are not to be found in standard dictionaries. For example, where would one find the words *pel-erpay* or *jonkha-erpay*? Even such a seemingly insignificant word as *bagicha* can be misconstrued if one is unfamiliar with the setting. So when Dhouli doesn't look up while she is sweeping the *bagicha*, she could be sweeping either a garden or an orchard depending upon what kind of *bagicha* usually surrounds a *malik mahajan's* residence.

I am deeply indebted to the author for going through my work with a fine-tooth comb. These stories were translated last year while I was on a Visiting Fellowship at the British Centre for Literary Translation, at the University of East Anglia. I shall always be thankful to everyone at BCLT for their friendship and for providing me with the time and space to think anew as a translator. And finally, thanks to all my colleagues at Seagull Books for keeping my spirits up.

November 2001

Dhouli

THE BUS LEFT RANCHI in the evening and reached Taharr around eight at night. The passengers got off in front of Parasnath's tea stall-cum-grocery shop and went to their respective homes. To Taharr, Parasnath's shop was Calcutta's Chowringhee or Darjeeling's Mall. The post office was next to it. The world beyond and the wide, metalled road ended here. Rohatgi Company's bus was the only link between Taharr and the rest of the world. The company had about 20 buses which plied up and down the Ranchi–Hazaribag, Ranchi–Ramgarh and Ranchi–Patna routes. They used poor, rundown buses for poor, rundown places like Taharr, Palani or Burudiha. The buses were crowded with adivasis on the local market days—Mondays, Wednesdays and Fridays. On Tuesdays, Thursdays, Saturdays and Sundays, they were empty. Empty buses didn't make money. The service was suspended during the rainy season as buses couldn't ply on unmetalled roads. Taharr would be completely cut off from the rest of the world during the monsoon months.

This year, it seemed the rains would arrive early, in June. Dhouli[1] was standing in front of Parasnath's shop. She could hardly be seen in the dim light of the store.

Parasnath shut his shop for the day and asked, Not going home? Dhouli turned her face away. Bother! Parasnath muttered and turned around to enter his house, behind the shop. His wife sat there smoking a *bidi*. Parasnath said, The girl's here again today.

She's had it.

If *deota*[2] gets wind of it . . .

Had it.

Then she said, When did Misrilal leave?

Nearly four months ago.

What does Dhouli expect? She's a *dusad*, an untouchable; did she expect a house and land?

God knows! But she's finished now.

Why?

That contractor! The coolie lines . . .

She'll get what's coming to her. A young woman . . . out alone at night . . . isn't she scared?

A wolf's been on the prowl since last night.

This was true. But Dhouli couldn't seem to keep it in mind. A terrible pain in her heart. In the middle of her chest. The pain would grow and push downwards. Dhouli didn't know what to do.

She returned home in the dark. A *dibri*[3] was burning. A *machan*[4] on one side of the room. Their bed. Three goats under it. Her mother was lying on the bed. She didn't speak to her daughter.

Dhouli checked the pitcher. It held some water. She drank some. She shut the door and blew out the *dibri*. Then she lay down beside her mother. Tears seeped from her eyes. Tears of deep despair. Her mother could hear; she understood everything. Dhouli kept crying. The night drew on, and her mother finally said, They'll throw us out.

Let them.

You are young. Where will I go?

You stay here.

You'll go?

Yes.

Where?

To hell.

Not that easy. People don't die at 19.

I will.

Did you go to Shanichari?

No! Dhouli screamed. Why should I? To get rid of the thorn in my womb? Never.

Will you see the Misras, then? Tell them, 'Your son has got me pregnant, give me money for the child's upkeep?'

How can I? Who will listen to me?

They'll have to.

If he was here, everything would be all right.

What does that mean? Would he have looked after you?

He said he would.

Does he know you're carrying his child?

Yes.

Would he have brought up the child?

He said so.

They always make such promises. You're not the first *dusad* girl the Misras have ruined. *Dusad*, *ganju*,[5] *dhobi*—who have they spared?

He's not like that.

Really? A brahman boy who knows fully well how things work here—why did he betray you?

He loves me.

Love! Is that why he's disappeared to Dhanbad for the past four months?

He's scared of his parents.

Couldn't even write a letter?

Can I read?

You fell in love, and I had to lose my cattle-grazing job. A wolf stole one of their lambs and they put the blame on me. Is that fair?

What can I do?

They were angry with you, so they punished me.

Throw me out then.

I will. Now go to sleep.

What did you say? You'll throw me out? Who else can you call your own?

They quarrelled every day over this and would have done so tonight. But they heard the watchman call out, Arrey, Dhouli *ki ma*! We have to hear your voice all day, now all night as well? All the others in the *dusadpatty*[6] know that the day is for yelling, the night for sleeping. Only you don't seem to realize this.

Okay, okay, I'll be quiet.

Have you let in some coolie or what?

May coolies enter *your* house!

Ram! Ram! How can you say such things?

The watchman left. Her mother said, Don't I know how this place works? Everyone's waiting to see if Misrilal takes care of you after the baby is born. If he does, no one will touch you. If not, they'll tear you to pieces.

Your mistake. Should have left me at my in-laws' after I was widowed. Left things to fate.

Did they want you? And you came away yourself.

My elder brother-in-law wouldn't have spared me.

And Misrilal did?

That hit Dhouli hard. She kept quiet. Her eyelids felt dry from crying endlessly. She shut them.

Sleep eludes her. Since the day Misrilal left. Since the day he crept off without a word, like a thief, on the early morning bus, Dhouli couldn't sleep. She could, of course, sleep forever by swallowing some of the insecticide used in the maize fields, but how could she die before seeing that traitor's face at least once more?

Traitor? No, no. Hadn't he left Taharr because his parents forced him to? Would his parents have been capable of threatening their beloved son? Hadn't the pressure applied by the head of their family, Hanuman Misra of Burudiha, scared them? Otherwise, would Misrilal have left Dhouli? How he had wept at the thought of leaving her! It broke her heart whenever she thought of it; even now she felt terrible.

Her mother tells her, Go get Shanichari's potion. Get rid of the thorn in your womb.

How can she? Was this the child of Misrilal's brother Kundan and Jhalo, the *ganju* girl? Born of greed and sheer lust?

Brahman, *deota*—Dhouli had never as much as raised her eyes to look at him, while sweeping their orchard. One afternoon, as she was bathing in the waterfall while grazing the goats in the forest, Misrilal tossed a leafy twig at her. He didn't laugh or make obscene comments. He simply said, I'm madly in love with you. Why won't you even look at me?

Deota! Please don't say such things.

Deota? I'm your slave.

Oh no! Please don't! Trembling in fear, Dhouli turned her face away.

You say no today, but some day you'll have to respond.

Whenever Dhouli remembers she can hear the breeze blowing through the trees in the forest, rustling leaves, the gurgling of the waterfall. That day, Misrilal had left it at that. How scared Dhouli felt, how scared! Misrilal was fair-skinned, he had curly hair. Innocent and goodlooking. At a glance you could make out that he was a *deota*. And what was Dhouli? A *dusad's* daughter. A widow. An unfortunate woman. She had no father or brother, which was why Kundan had not let her mother till the land. Dhouli's mother had pleaded, *Sarkar*, I'll pay the rent; the other *dusads* will help me till the land. I'll pay whatever rent you ask but give me the land. Otherwise we'll starve to death.

No.

Dhouli's mother then went and prostrated herself before Kundan's mother. Help us, Mataji.[7] Or my daughter and I will die of starvation.

The mother told her son, As long as her husband was alive he tilled the land and worked as bonded labour. Is she to starve to death now that she is a widow?

What can I do? I've given that land to Jhuman *dusad*.

Then they'll graze the goats, sweep the orchard. You'll pay for that and give them *maroa*.

Whatever you say.

Why had a son of the family on whom they had to depend for their meagre daily bowl of *maroa* said such things to Dhouli? She knew it was because of her tremulous eyes, her slender waist, her blossoming breasts. Still she went to sweep the orchard, keeping herself carefully covered with her coarse sari, bought at the local market. She never lifted her eyes to look around at the fruit-laden trees. Took home only the guavas and custard apples that were half-eaten by the birds and lambs. That, too, with permission from Kundan's mother.

Dhouli went home and polished their brass plate until it shone like gold. Then she looked at the reflection of her face. Careful not to let her mother see. After becoming a widow, a *randi*,[8] you were not supposed to look in a mirror. Not supposed to look at yourself. Not supposed to wear shellac bangles, a dot of sindoor on your forehead, anklets of cheap metal. She was attractive. But a pretty face was no use to a *randi*. She couldn't marry again, could she? Never again would the other girls call her to sing wedding songs like *sasural chale sita maiya* or paint *rangoli* patterns of birds and flowers on the walls of a bride's home. Yet the younger son of that brahman family had just told her he was her slave. She felt scared, uneasy.

Dhouli told her mother, Ma, you sweep the orchard; I'll graze the goats.

Why?

Ma, the leaves keep flying around when I'm sweeping, and I can't run around after them.

Has someone said something?

Of course not.

Don't go deep into the forest with the goats. Wolves and leopards roam there.

Of course I won't, Ma! I know better than that!

While grazing the goats in the forest, memories of long ago come flooding back. Of going to the mela riding on her father's shoulders. Of returning home with a mere paisa's worth of *tilua*[9] after watching people buy and sell goods worth lakhs of rupees. Before Dhouli left her in-laws' place to come back to her mother, she had worked as a helping hand on the *mahajan*'s farm. They had two broken-down rooms; her mother-in-law would boil some corn at the end of the day. They would sit down to eat after the men had finished their meal.

Dhouli did not remember getting married. She was too young then. When her body blossomed, she had her *gouna*[10] and went to live with her husband. Her father had to borrow from the Misras for her wedding and the *gouna*. He died repaying that loan, working for them as a bonded labourer.

Her husband was no good. He would beat her. He died of fever. Her mother-in-law had said, You'll have to work hard at your mother's. The same as here.

Dhouli knew that was life. Wearing coarse, dull plain black cloth, and slaving on the *mahajan*'s farm or the *jotedar*'s fields or doing road construction work. Barely managing one square meal before lying down beside her mother-in-law at the end of the day. But her husband's elder brother from Bhalatore landed up. Began eyeing her. Her mother-in-law didn't know what to do. So Dhouli came away. She had one regret; she hadn't got to see the *nautanki*. A troupe was to have visited their village. The *mahajan* had commissioned a performance.

After returning to Taharr, she hadn't encouraged any of the young *dusad* men. The same poverty and hunger. The same back-breaking labour. On top of that, a child too? No, she didn't want such a life.

She thought of many such things while grazing goats in the forest. Sometimes she would lie down and rest, spreading the end of her sari on the ground. She wasn't scared of wolves or leopards. If men were afraid of animals, so were animals afraid of man. The forest was peaceful. She was almost over the uneasiness caused by Misrilal's words. She was at peace.

But there was a mela at Jhujhar. While returning, Dhouli fell behind her group. She was anxiously hurrying back home. Flesh traders were known to visit such rural fairs. They always managed to smuggle out a few women.

It was on the way home that Misrilal caught up with her. He said, Didn't you hear me?

What?

I was calling you.

Why?

Don't you know?

No. *Deota*, don't say such things. I'm a *dusadin* and you are a *deota*.

I love you.

No, *deota*. Don't call it love. You're a brahman, you're a young man. You'll soon get married, your bride will come . . .

It's you I . . . *dusadin*, don't you understand what love means?

No, *deota*. *Dusads* and *ganjus* like us bear your children, it's not unusual, but . . .

I can't think of anything but you.

Please don't play with a poor woman like me, *sarkar*.

Play?

Yes, *deota*. You'll play your games and push off, but what will happen to me? Look what happened to Jhalo! And Shanichari! No, *sarkar*!

And what if I don't let you go?

What can I do? Nothing. *Deotas* like you always get what you want! Go ahead, take me, dishonour me.

No, no, Dhouli. Forgive me, please forgive me.

Misrilal left hastily. Dhouli was stunned. She returned home.

The day she heard that Misrilal was very ill—lovesick—Dhouli felt it deeply. Misrilal could take her whenever he wished, the Misras did it all the time, and Dhouli couldn't have resisted. But what kind of behaviour was this?

Dhouli felt confused. Then one day the village women got hold of her near the well.

Randi, fortune's smiling on you.

Can a *randi* ever be lucky?

Deota's younger son is crazy for you.

Lies.

We all know about it.

Don't lie.

Why should we? Everyone knows now.

No, no!

A distracted Dhouli fetched water and came away, then went into the forest with the goats. What would happen to her now?

The whole village knew. Would they spare her? Why did *deota* have to lose his head?

She was too scared to go anywhere near the Misra household. Her mother told her he was being treated. A doctor had come from Bhalatore. Dhouli can't make out whether her mother knew what the women at the well knew.

One day she told her mother, Let's go to Bhalatore, Ma. We'll work as coolies.

Are you crazy?

Then she heard that Misrilal was better. He would be getting married soon. They were on the lookout for a good-looking girl. For his elder brother Kundan, the family had not sought a pretty match. This time it seems they were looking for a beauty.

She was very relieved. At the same time it hurt somewhere. And yet, a sense of triumph. She, Dhouli, a *dusad* girl, had driven a brahman's son crazy.

It was with an easy mind that she went into the forest and bathed herself under the waterfall. She spread her sari to dry on a rock, then wrapped it around her, still damp. It was ragged with use. Dhouli would have to buy another the next time her mother got paid. Ma would have been livid had she seen Dhouli in a wet blouse and damp sari. She would have said, Are you a widow or a streetwalking *randi*? Showing off your body?

That was when Misrilal came up to her, saying, I don't want to get married, Dhouli. I want only you.

In the forest bordering their village, the afternoons were primordial, languorous. Dhouli's mind and body were caught off guard. Misrilal's eyes were helpless and pleading, his voice aching with despair. Dhouli could no longer refuse him.

The next two months were like an enchanted dream. The forest was their meeting place, the afternoons their appointed hour. All caution was swept away in a flood of passion. Nineteen and 23. Each time, Dhouli would tremble in fear. What will happen?

Happen to what?

You'll get married.

To you.

Don't say that, *deota*.

I don't care about things like caste and untouchability. Besides, Taharr is not the only place on earth. And the government law too sanctions our marriage.

Don't say that, *sarkar*. You're still young, immature. What will your father and Hanumanji say to all this? They'll drive us out of the village.

It's not that easy. The law of the land is with us.

Not for us, it isn't.

You don't know.

Misrilal would avow such daring plans in the privacy of the secluded forest and his words, interwoven with the fables and fairytales of the forest, would take on an unreal, magical aura.

Time could have stopped for them. But it did not. Dhouli realized that she was pregnant.

Strangely, Misrilal was very happy. He said, I'm as illiterate as you are. I have no interest in owning these lands and orchards. We'll go to Dhanbad via Bhalatore and from there to Patna. We'll open a shop and earn our living.

But the day Hanuman Misra came to Taharr, Misrilal was unable to utter a word before him.

Kundan said, We'll kill them both, mother and daughter, and get rid of the bodies.

No.

Hanuman Misra said, First clean up your own house. The garbage outside will automatically vanish.

We'll kill them.

Fool!

Her mother, that bitch, raised a hue and cry saying a wolf had stolen the lamb. How come they have three goats in their hut? They used to have two.

Misraji was furious. You silly ass. It's better to talk to your wife than to you.

Forgive me, please.

Don't bother murdering them, deny them food instead. Sack them. And remember, your brother has brought shame to the entire family. People are laughing at us. First, restore our honour. How does it matter if we have one less goat? You big goat, you! Look, first send your brother away.

Misrilal said, I'm not going anywhere.

If you don't go, we'll make sure your corpse leaves the village. Men like you are a black mark against our name.

Later, in desperation, Misrilal told his mother, Ma, Dhouli is carrying my child.

So what? The men of our family have planted their seed in so many *dusad* and *ganju* girls. You're a hot-blooded young man. Even Jhalo has three sons by Kundan.

What will she do?

She has sinned. She'll suffer for it. They'll both starve to death, mother and daughter.

How is she to blame, Ma?

It's always the fault of the woman. For not considering a brahman's honour, she's even more to blame.

Ma, you love me, don't you?

Aren't you my baby boy?

Swear by me.

Why?

Please.

Okay.

I'll obey you all, I'll go away. But promise me that you'll ensure she doesn't starve to death.

I . . . promise.

And that no one will harass her.

All right.

If you don't keep your promise Ma . . . you know me, I may not be able to speak up in front of *Deota* but you know how stubborn I can be. I swear I'll never return or get married if you fail to keep your word.

No, no. Don't say that, please. I'll look after the *dusadin* and . . . provide for them.

Dhouli found out about it. It never occurred to her to protest. This was not the first time that a brahman's son had ruined a *dusad*'s daughter. Their village society held Dhouli solely responsible. Her kinsfolk rejected her because she had fallen in love. She had kept aloof from the men of her community. That was all right. If Misrilal had used force, they would not have spurned her. There were several illegitimate Misra children growing up in the *dusad–ganju–*

dhobi quarters. But Dhouli had been willing. An unforgivable offence. The *dusad–ganju* lads and the contractor's coolies were watching closely to see how the situation developed. Sometimes the Misras looked after the mothers of their illegitimate children by giving them work or money or food. Such women and their children were treated well by the villagers. Otherwise, the Misras would be offended. And if that happened no one would be spared. They thought, if the Misras provided for Dhouli, they would forget about the entire episode. Otherwise they would see to it that Dhouli, the *randi*, the widow, was forced into prostitution.

Dhouli was aware of all this and knew what would happen. Fear and sorrow overwhelmed her. Suddenly the forest lost all its charm; the trees were ghostly sentries; even the rocks seemed to watch her. She waited in vain near the waterfall. Misrilal didn't come.

Finally he came. When Dhouli was exhausted and drained from waiting for him, Misrilal appeared. She looked at him and read her death sentence. Dhouli buried her face in Misrilal's chest and wept inconsolably. He too wept, his face in her hair. The scent of soap. Misrilal used to bring her soap and fragrant oil. Bought her two saris as well. They were printed saris, so Dhouli never wore them. A strange emptiness filled Misrilal.

Dhouli, my beloved, why were you born a *dusadin*?

Don't say that, *deota*. Please don't. I can't take it any more.

Listen. Crying won't help you now.

I have a whole lifetime to cry.

This time I have to leave. I've had to accept all their conditions.

Why did you talk of love?

I still love you.

Sarkar! Your Dhouli is dead now. Please don't laugh at the dead, *sarkar*.

Listen to me, you silly girl.

Misrilal made her sit on a rock. He lifted her face up and said, I'll stay quiet for a month. I won't be pressured into marriage, I've told them that and they've agreed.

You'll forget me.

Of course not. Listen, I'll return in a month's time. By then I'll have decided where to go and what to do. I am not an educated guy. I don't want a good job. Nor do I want all the land and property like my elder brother. I'll settle somewhere and open a shop. These things have to be arranged, after all.

What should I do?

You stay here.

How will we survive? Your brother called Ma a thief and sacked her.

My mother has sworn that she'll look after you and your needs. Besides . . .

Misrilal tied five 10-rupee notes to the end of Dhouli's sari. He told her, Be brave for a month.

Then he left. After caressing her and reassuring her. She returned home after a while. Mother and daughter talked things over, then put the notes in a jar and buried it under the floor.

Misrilal left the village. After a couple of days Dhouli's mother went to the Misra house. Without a word, the mistress of the house doled out a kilogram of *maroa*, careful to avoid touching her. She told Dhouli's mother, Come back after three days.

On her next visit, the quantity of *maroa* was halved but the three-day frequency remained unchanged. The third time Misrilal's mother grimly told her, Since you were here last I haven't been able to find the *lota*[11] for storing milk.

But Maiya, I never . . .

No, my elder son has asked me not to let you in the house. Stay near the door and call me.

Without a word of protest Dhouli's mother left the place. But when she stood outside and called on her next visit, she was told that Maiya had left for Burudiha. For Hanuman Misra's house. Dhouli's mother returned home furious and beat her daughter mercilessly. Dhouli did not utter a word. After her mother finally gave up, Dhouli handed her a sickle. She said, Here, use this. Your hands must be tired. Besides, just one stroke will do the trick. It's very sharp.

Mother and daughter held each other and began to weep. Then the mother said, I'm telling you for your own good. Ask Shanichari to give you a potion.

Why?

Get rid of the thorn in your womb.

No, Ma.

He's not going to come back. Too immature. He may have thought he could keep his word but he won't be able to. It's not possible.

I'll poison myself if he doesn't return.

Will you?

Yes.

Her mother kept quiet for some time. Then she sighed and said, Let me go to that contractor, the forest contractor. He once asked me to cook for him.

Shall I go?

No, no, I'm old now, I'll go. Even if he doesn't pay he'll give me food. And I'll bring it home.

You go then.

You graze the goats.

That's how they worked things out. Dhouli's mother didn't get a cook's job but she worked as a helper. The day she got something to eat, she brought it home. The *dusads* kept a close watch on the mother and daughter. So did the coolies. They felled trees. Got paid in cash. But she's Kundan's brother's kept woman, that's the problem. They were keen to see what would happen ultimately. Felling trees and transporting the wood to cities would go on for a long time. Waiting was not a problem for them. Rather, it held a kind of excitement. Since Dhouli was involved with a brahman's son, her attraction seemed to have doubled.

One month, two months, four months passed. Every day, Dhouli would return home after waiting for the bus. Today, lying on the *machan*, she relived everything. Every little detail. Then she shut her eyes. Put her hand on her belly. The baby kicked. Strange *sensayshun*. Misrilal had said if it was a boy he would name it Murari. But somehow Misrilal and his love were beginning to seem as unreal as a fairytale. Dhouli's son was born at the end of Ashwin. Shanichari was the midwife. She cut the cord. She said, It's Dhouli's child, that's why he's so fair.

Earlier, Dhouli's mother had spoken to Shanichari. Dhouli had to be given a potion to make her infertile. Shanichari gave her something. She said, It's very bitter but it will do you a lot of good.

Dhouli's mother asked, She won't die, will she?

No, no. I gave the same medicine to Kundan Misra's wife. She didn't die, did she?

It won't harm her?

No.

I hope so.

What are you going to do now?

Leave it to God.

Misrilal is getting married.

Shshhh . . . Dhouli will hear you.

What next?

Whatever is to happen will happen.

They'll stone your door.

I know.

Misrilal will be sent to Dhanbad after the wedding. They've set up a cycle shop for him there.

I had warned Dhouli.

I told you earlier that if the *deotas* don't provide for Dhouli, I'll send the forest overseer to your place.

Let's not discuss this now.

Shanichari was the village gossip and medicine woman, so the Misras left her alone. She was somehow moved by Dhouli's plight and, in her typical manner, decided to raise public opinion in the girl's favour.

She went to treat Misrilal's mother for rheumatic pain and told her, Dhouli's had a son.

So?

Looks exactly like your son.

Says who? That's a lie.

Come now. We all know that your son was in love with her. So many of your offspring are born to our women, does anyone sit in judgement?

Since you've brought it up . . .

Yes?

Can you make them leave this place?

Where will they go?

Anywhere. Misrilal's would-be in-laws are a renowned family, and the bride's not all that young. If they get to hear of this, they'll be annoyed.

Part with some money and they'll leave.

How much?

A thousand.

Let me see. I'll talk to my elder son.

You didn't support her, didn't provide for her. That really gave you a bad name. Haven't your husband and elder son fooled around with *ganju* girls? They've always been provided for. What happened this time to make you turn your face away and act so pious?

Dhouli's mother stole a *lota* . . .

That's not true, Maiya.

So what should I do now?

Misra's wife tolerated Shanichari because of her potions, which helped keep her old and promiscuous husband under control.

Do something for them.

Let me speak to my elder son.

Her elder son Kundan said, Forget it. She's just had a son. Soon she'll start taking in clients, the slut. I'll take care of things at this end—even when Misrilal gets married, he won't come to the village.

His mother was most relieved to hear this and forgot all about Dhouli.

But Hanumanji objected, That won't do. After the marriage, the bride must first come home and then they can leave for Dhanbad together. Why shouldn't they come to the village? For fear of that *dusad* woman? What can she do?

Dhouli heard all the news. She sat at home with her son, thinking things over. Her mother could lose her job any day. Dhouli and the infant were dependent on her. They could perhaps sell off the goats, one by one. But could they live off that? For how long? And after that? After that?

The very thought of Misrilal made her mind go numb. Did all that love, all those words, mean nothing? No, it couldn't be. The forest and the waterfall had always been the source of numerous legends. A fairy was apparently seen there on full moon nights. The famous daroga Mukkhan Singh was said to have gone mad at the sight of her. It seemed so unreal, so magical, that tale. The *ganju* girl Jhulni had fallen in love with her brother-in-law and the panchayat had driven both of them to suicide—they had gone into the forest and swallowed the poisonous seeds of the *kolke* flower. Dhouli had known them both, yet the whole story seemed unreal to her, the stuff of legend. In that very forest, near the same waterfall, once upon a time, had a brahman boy whispered sweet nothings to a *dusad* girl, murmuring, You are my *koyeli*,[12] my beautiful dark bride? Had they lain wrapped in each other's arms on a bed of red flowers strewn on that forest floor? Had it really happened? Had a *deota* really kissed the feet of a *dusadin* after extracting a thorn from it one day? No, it couldn't have been. It was all a fantasy! Only the child sleeping in her lap was real.

So Misrilal couldn't honour his word. Dhouli had nothing to say. But what was she to do now? Would Misrilal feel compassion on seeing his child? Would he give her some land to till?

The Misras had done so before, hadn't they?

Dhouli's mind said no.

Would clients then start knocking at her door and after saying 'no' a few times, would she ultimately succumb to hunger and let them in? For the sake of a sari from someone, a few coins from someone else, some *maroa* from a third?

Dhouli's mind said no.

How could Dhouli even fetch water from the well? All the women would be busy talking about Misrilal's *baraat* and wedding. When the *baraat* enters the village, even *dusad* girls sing and dance at a distance. They are given *laddoo, chira, chhatu*[13] as well as money at the Misra house. But how could Dhouli take part in the dance? How could she sing, *Mai nachaot mai gawat baraat aiyo rey*?

What will Dhouli do?

After giving the mistress of the Misra family a piece of her mind, Shanichari went off to the *dusad* neighbourhood. She told them, *Deota*'s son brought shame on Dhouli. And all of you looked the other way. What's to become of the girl?

No one's brought shame on Dhouli. She was in love. And she spurned the men of her own caste. We are not interested in what happens to her. Let her do what she can.

What is she to do?

Let's wait and see what her beloved *deota* does for her, how well he looks after her!

Misrilal did nothing. He didn't even raise his head as he entered the village, leading the *baraat*. No lamps were lit at Dhouli's home. New clothes, sweets, liquor were freely distributed in the *dusad*, *ganju* and *dhobi* neighbourhoods. The village had never seen such an ostentatious wedding before. Dhouli sat near the waterfall in the forest, waiting and waiting. In vain. Misrilal never turned up.

Dhouli fell at Shanichari's feet.

Shanichari came back from the Misra house and said, He's very upset.

Why?

You refused to accept the arrangements his mother made for both of you.

Did he say so?

Yes.

Then you'd better tell him to come here. Say that if he doesn't, I'll take his son and go to his wife. Even if the chief *deota* kills me for it.

Misrilal arrived. Spoke not a word. Eyes full of questions. Dhouli knew. He was still attracted to her. It felt good. Sometimes, a sense of triumph could make one merciless and force out the bitter truth.

Did you tell Shanichari that we refused the dole your mother was handing out?

That's what my mother told me.

Thuu! I spit on such lies! Your mother handed out something like two kilos of *maroa*, that too once in 10 days. Then she called my mother a thief and chased her away.

I didn't know.

Why did you ruin my life?

I love you . . .

Thuu! To hell with your love! If you had taken me by force, I could've got an acre of land. But you're not even a man! Your brother's a man! He gave Jhalo sons and he also gave her a house and land. What did you do for me?

Whatever I did was against my wishes.

You can get married, get a shop set up for you, all to please others! But to please yourself it seems you can only ruin the poor! My people too have turned against me now all because of you!

I'll give you . . .

Money? How much? Give me what I need to bring up your son.

I'll send it to you from the shop.

You're lying.

I will, I promise.

We'll see.

For now . . .

Hand it over.

Dhouli tied the 100 rupee note to the end of her sari. Then she said, A hundred rupees won't go far even in Taharr these days. I was doomed the day I got involved with you. If you don't send me money, I'll go to Dhanbad and leave your son with you.

Go on. I'll have to accept whatever you say.

You've ruined my life, *deota*. Does it hurt to hear a few home truths? Or are all rich people like you so thin-skinned?

Dhouli came away. Told her mother, Go to Bhalatore and speak to Mausi. We'll shift there and if necessary, I'll sell myself there.

Bold words.

Yes. If I have to disgrace myself, I'll do it there. Not here.

Will you get more money there?

How should I know?

The next day Misrilal left for Dhanbad with his wife. While they were boarding the bus, his wife's brother asked, Who's that girl?

Where?

That one there with the baby. Staring at you.

Dhouli. With her son in her arms.

A *dusad* woman.

So attractive?

Maybe. I didn't notice.

The bus began its journey.

Some people live to see most of their dreams come true. But Dhouli's life held no hope. Such lives never do. Her aunt offered no encouragement. The 100 rupees that Misrilal had given Dhouli were soon spent on food. Only nine rupees were left. He sent no word, nor any money. Although they later heard that he had once sent 20 rupees through a truck driver who pocketed it. Dhouli's mother lost a goat. She had to sell the other two and as always, because the seller was needy, it went cheap.

Dhouli realized that her community, the Misra family and the contractor's labourers, would watch her keenly now. They could see that her son was growing up on scraps and scrapings. They knew that her mother searched for roots and tubers in the forest. They were aware that Shanichari visited them sometimes with *makai*[14] tied to her waistcloth. Seeing all this they realized that Misrilal had washed his hands off the whole thing.

One night Dhouli could hear someone pelting stones at her door.

Whoever you are, I sleep with a *baloa*[15] beside me, Dhouli screamed. Someone whistled and left.

More stones. Dhouli pretended not to hear. Again.

Fuck your mother and sisters, she shouted.

Her mother mumbled, How long will you keep them away?

As long as I can.

I can't take it any longer.

Nor can I, Ma.

What shall we do?

Can't we move to a city and take to begging?

Who'll give us alms? And the men will be after you there too.

Do I still look like something men will want?

Why else the stones?

For the sake of the child . . .

I can't bear it any more. You and your son. Else I would have gone to Shanichari long ago.

I'll do something tomorrow.

What?

Work as a field hand.

People do it every day. How much will you get? Almost nothing.

Let me see.

Next morning Dhouli went to Parasnath's shop and said, At least let me earn something by sweeping this place. We are starving to death!

Parasnath told her, Here's some *maroa*. Take it and leave. I don't need a helping hand. If I give you a job, the *deota* will be annoyed with me.

Why? What have I done to him?

Because of his brother.

Dhouli tied the *maroa* to the end of her sari and sat in the shade of a tree. If Kundan Misra didn't kill her physically, he would finish her off by denying her food. That was her punishment for loving his brother. How long would this *maroa* last? Even if cooked as a watery gruel?

Her mother didn't say a word when she saw Dhouli return with the *maroa*. But when it was time to eat, she served them and said, You and your beloved son can have it. I'm leaving. I'll go where the road takes me. Can't starve to death like this.

Won't you eat?

No. Wretched female, if you can't do anything else, why don't you kill yourself!

Yes. I will.

Dhouli tried that too. Tried drowning herself under that very same waterfall. If she died, the community would look after her mother. As for the child, if Dhouli's mother was able to take care of him, he would live. Or he'd die too.

But she couldn't do it. That man in a printed lungi and shirt—the head coolie—took her by the hand. He said, So? Where's your *baloa*?

Dhouli looked him straight in the eye. Fearlessly.

Let go.

He let go of her hand.

You came to my door?

Yes.

The man made an obscene gesture. Dhouli realized that this was her fate. She paused, sighed, and then said, All right.

Will you let me in?

Yes. And . . .

Yes?

Bring some money.

Money?

Yes. And some *makai* too. If I'm setting up shop, I might as well charge.

Dhouli returned home. Told her mother, Go and sleep with Shanichari from tonight. Take the baby with you.

Why?

They'll come. I'll let them in.

Dhouli's mother might have started to cry, but Dhouli spoke impatiently, Don't raise a hue and cry. Come back quietly before dawn.

That night Dhouli inaugurated one of the printed saris that Misrilal had given her. She borrowed some oil from Shanichari and rubbed it into her scalp. Took a bath, groomed her hair. What else ought she to do? There must be more.

That night there was a rap on their door. The man brought *makai*, dal, salt and a rupee. Dhouli gave him his money's worth and said, Never come empty-handed.

Don't let anyone else in.

Whoever is ready to pay can come.

There were many ready to pay. They kept coming. Dhouli and her mother wore proper clothes again. Ate two square meals a day. Dhouli felt very sleepy these days, after her clients left. How simple to sell one's body in a loveless exchange for salt, corn, *maroa*. If she had known it was that easy, she would have done it much earlier. Her son too would have been well fed, healthy. Dhouli thought she had really been too naive.

There was somebody else watching all this. Kundan. He realized it was a case of the survival of the fittest. Dhouli had learnt to survive, had bested his attempt at vengeance. Kundan was burning with rage. That *dusadin* had become such a coveted female.

One day, seeing Dhouli fetch water from the well, Kundan told Shanichari, You drink water from the same well she uses?

Who?

That Dhouli.

What is it to you, *deota*? Everyone frequents her these days. We've accepted her . . .

Why?

Why not? How is she at fault?

She's become a *randi*.

She was a widow. But your brother forced her to become a prostitute. If she hadn't, would your brother's son have survived? Everyone seems to be happy now. Even your friend, the contractor. His coolies no longer wander off here and there for a bit of fun.

Your tongue is getting sharper by the day!

That's enough. If it wasn't for me, your mother and wife wouldn't be alive today.

Kundan realized that he had been defeated. He went home without saying a word. Shanichari was indispensable to the village. People depended on her medicines.

Kundan went to Dhanbad and threatened his younger brother. Either give her some land, or some money. Because of you we now have a whore in the village!

What!

Misrilal paled. Kundan was secretly delighted. His brother still had a soft spot for that female! And Kundan had succeeded in rubbing salt in his wound! *Shabash*![16] This brother of his was not man enough! He was not even proud to be a brahman! A man should be a man! If Kundan had been the younger brother, would he have given up his woman on the say-so of Hanuman Misra? But this one had done just that! He had to be made into a man! Untouchables must always be kept totally under control; at times one could take pity on them but one must be a man! Otherwise how would Kundan manage it all? So many fields, orchards, illegitimate offspring, sexy, lowcaste females! Such bliss! How else would he manage his empire?

Want to know why? That sweetheart of yours, that damned *dusad* woman! Fell in love with a brahman and became the mother of a son! And now, he made an obscene gesture, the door through which the lion entered is being visited by rats and swine!

No. Never!

Yes. And everyone's laughing at us brahmans!

Can't be.

A hundred times yes! Sissy! Coward! Why couldn't you tell Hanumanji to his face that you wanted her as your kept woman? Jhalo's my mistress! Hanumanji didn't want me to give her land or a house. Did I listen to him? *Thuu*! To hell with your love! Falling for a *dusad* girl! You should have fun and at the same time keep everyone under your control, from the panchayat to the *prajas*.[17] Sissy! Faggot! You've brought shame on all us brahmans!

I must see it with my own eyes. Only then will I believe you! If it's a lie . . .

Kundan smiled a sly, triumphant smile. Kill me! I got you a gun license, didn't I?

Misrilal came to Taharr burning with rage and venom. There was no Dhouli waiting for him at the bus stop, she didn't see him arrive.

He knocked on Dhouli's door that evening and, draped in a red sari with green bangles, hair smoothly oiled and braided, a new Dhouli opened the door to him.

At the sight of Misrilal, her face went pale. But instantly she grew hard and composed. In a cold voice she said, *Deota*! *Sarkar*! Do you wish to come in?

Misrilal came in. A lantern instead of a *dibri*. A fresh rug and pillow on the *machan*. Stored under it, a sack of *maroa* and a container of oil.

You've become a whore?

Of course.

Why?

You left after you'd had your fun. Your elder brother tried to kill us by denying us food. I had to save your son and myself.

Why didn't you die instead!

I tried to kill myself. But then I thought, why should I? You can get married, run a shop, see movies with your wife, and I have to kill myself? Why? Why? Why?

I'll kill you!

Do it.

A brahman's son to be brought up by *acchuts*! Untouchables! I'll kill you!

You aren't man enough!

Don't say that, Dhouli, don't call me a sissy! My elder brother said the same thing! Don't you start! I'll show you that I'm both a man and a brahman's son too!

Misrilal, Kundan and Hanumanji summoned a panchayat meeting within a few days. People were not asked their opinion at the meeting. Hanumanji announced, Dhouli cannot practise prostitution in this village. She can go to some town, to Ranchi, and do her whoring there. If not, her house will be set on fire and mother, daughter, child will be burned to death. Such sinful activities cannot continue in the heart of this village. This village still has brahmans living in it. Puja is still done in their homes every day.

Dhouli asked, Why didn't the brahmans pay for the upkeep of one of their own offspring?

Hanuman Misra took off his shoe and flung it at her, saying, Shut up, *randi*!

Misrilal said, Now you know that I'm a man and that I'm also a brahman's son!

The *dusads*, *ganjus* and others didn't challenge the verdict. But where was Ranchi? How would Dhouli get there?

Kundan said, My contractor will take her there. Tomorrow.

Early next morning, Dhouli and the contractor took a bus. A bundle in Dhouli's hand. Dry tearless eyes. Totally shattered. As if her mind had stopped functioning. Mechanical movements. A puppet. Controlled by the will of others.

Her mother stood there with the baby in her arms, weeping inconsolably. The child stretched out his little arms to his mother. Dhouli said softly, Keep some *gur* with you. If he cries at night, put some into his mouth.

Her mother let out a cry. It would have been better if you had just stayed with your brother-in-law! Dhouli's face broke into an inscrutable, pitying smile. If that had been the case, she would have been a *randi* in her private life. But now she was about to become a professional *randi*. When you are a kept woman, you're all alone. But now she would be part of a community. The collective strength of that society was far more powerful than an individual's strength. And those who had forced her to be a whore were the ones who controlled society. They were the most powerful! Her mother wouldn't understand all this, but Dhouli did. Which is why she could smile and say, Keep some *gur* for him. And leave a lamp lit, he's scared of the dark.

The bus driver working for Rohatgi Company couldn't look Dhouli in the face. He blew the horn and started the bus. Dhouli refused to look back because if she did, she would see the brass trident atop the temple of the Misras.

Kundan's contractor couldn't face Dhouli either. Eyes averted, he said, Rest a little. Ranchi is a long way off.

The bus picked up speed. The distance between Ranchi and Dhouli was gradually being bridged. The sun shone brightly. The sky looked blue and the trees as green as always. She realized that nature was unaffected by the upheaval in her life. This painful thought made her weep. Wasn't everything supposed to change from today? Everything? The day Dhouli was to finally enter the marketplace? Or is it that, for girls like Dhouli, nature accepted such a fate as only natural? The nature which, after all, was not created by the Misras—or had the sky, the trees and the earth sold out to the Misras as well?

Shanichari

WHEN SHANICHARI WAS A GIRL OF 12, she went to the *haat* in Tohri. And why not? After all, they enjoyed the train ride to Tohri, sitting on the floor of the compartment, chugging along, having a good time picking the lice from each other's hair. Shanichari had gone with her grandmother, her *eng-ajji*. *Eng-ajji* knew all sorts of age-old tales and stories. She didn't often find a willing audience. The old woman could hardly hear, but she loved telling stories.

After they got on to the train, Shanichari settled her grandmother with her back against a wall. She said, Thakuma, tell us that story about the foolish son-in-law. It'll pass the time.

That one? All right.

Go on, start.

The foolish son-in-law was on his way to his in-laws'. He walked and walked and walked. Suddenly—who's following him? Must be another man going the same way. Didn't realize it was his shadow. So the stupid man offered the shadow a *pithey*[1] and said, 'Here, eat this.'

Shanichari collapsed with laughter at this point. What a fool! Offering food to his own shadow! But *eng-ajji* never managed to finish a story. She would fall asleep half-way.

Oh, Thakuma, sleeping again?

Then the sindoorwalla said, 'I'll marry the girl. I've given her sindoor. And so she's mine.'

Which story is that?

Why? Don't you know the one about the carpenter who carved a girl out of wood and became her father? The weaver who gave her clothes and became her brother? The goldsmiths who gifted her jewellery and became her uncles? Didn't the sindoorwalla bring her to life by giving her sindoor?

You mean the story of the four friends?

How would you know it? Nice story, isn't it? When we were young, the boys would all go to the *jonkha-erpay*[2] and we girls would go to the *pel-erpay.*[3] Stay up all night listening to stories. Singing songs. Those were the days.

The old woman had fallen asleep again. Shanichari was leaning against the window. How wonderful it was, this freedom! Today she didn't have to graze the goats, pick firewood or cook the rice. She could just run free. Outside the window, trees-huts-fields-hills streamed past her and Shanichari felt as if she was rushing ahead.

Hey, careful! Don't stick your head out of the window.

Hiralal called out to her. Hiralal wandered from train to train with a harmonium around his neck, singing songs. No one knew how old he was. Even women who were mothers several times over could remember him unchanged. Hiralal's address—the shade of a tree, the side of a road. He had a wizened look, a shabby shirt and pants, a pair of slippers.

Startled, Shanichari drew back.

You'll get coal dust in your eyes.

Shanichari didn't reply.

Come, sit here. Aren't you Moti Linda's daughter?

Yes.

I know. From Chotti *tehsil*,[4] aren't you?

Yes.

I keep track of everyone. Mongru who got jailed was from your village, no? Is he free now?

Oh yes, ages back.

Didn't the panchayat meet? On his return from jail, didn't he feast you all? Is it all over?

Shanichari shook her head. Mongru went off to Kolkatta. Said he'd earn some money, come home and then treat us.

Kolkatta?

Yes, yes. Many of them have left.

Where to?

To the brick kilns.

A plump female wrapped in a yellow sari had been dozing all this while. She woke up now. Yawning, she said, Good for them. Why starve to death in the village?

Gohuman Bibi, is it you?

Who the hell are you?

Look carefully, you've seen me before.

Oh! Hiralal

Where are you off to?

Tohri *haat*.

Fishing again?

Enough of your jokes.

I'm not joking. You must have cast your net already. Nandi must have been sent ahead to find out everything. When you arrive she'll tell you the number of girls per village. You'll go back to Kolkatta and get the requisite amount of money from the *malik*. Come back and treat the villagers to a slap-up meal of meat and rice, throw in liquor too. Tell the girls, why bother starving to death here? Come with me. Work in the brick kilns. Come to Kolkatta. You'll make money, get new saris.

So? Don't I find them work in the brick kilns?

You're Gohuman all right![5] A cobra spits venom, like you. You sell off the girls. Twenty rupees per girl. Supply a thousand girls and make 20,000.

What about cuts? Me, a cobra? It's the *malik* who's the snake. His musclemen take money from me.

What you're doing is a terrible sin, don't you know that?

Gohuman shook her head. She said, What do you mean, sin? What kind of sin? What makes you so holier-than-thou? She began counting on her fingers and said, Wait a minute. Let me explain. The *malik* runs a brick kiln. He needs *rejas*.[6] Is he committing a sin? He's running a business, you get me? A business.

Yes, of course, and you're his *paatnar*.

I'm just supplying him *rejas*. These girls don't get enough to eat, I'm finding them jobs. What sin am I committing?

Thuu! I spit on your kind of work. You witch. You first became the *malik*'s whore, and now you're making them whores too.

The blame lies elsewhere. Perhaps with you people. Why else would there be such poverty here?

Are you saying there's poverty because of us?

Oh . . . I can't carry on arguing with you.

What else can you say?

Who's this girl?

Shanichari, who had been gaping at them all this while, started. Hiralal spoke warningly, Don't look at her. Listen, girl! Call your grandmother or whoever she is. We've almost reached Tohri. And listen, if this Gohuman Bibi enters your village, drive her out.

Gohuman smiled and said, We'll see. I've heard such threats before.

She's as poisonous as a cobra.

Huh . . . look who's talking. Sings for his supper, and talks like a hero!

Shanichari's grandmother suddenly woke up in the middle of all this. Immediately she began, And then the king said . . .

Shanichari said, We're almost there. Let's get off. No more stories.

We've reached?

Here we are.

Gohuman Bibi had begun singing,

Come with me, all you girls,
To Kolkatta we'll go,
Riding on a train,
Come on, off we go.

The hustle and bustle of the Tohri *haat* started right at the station. Shanichari got off the train holding tight to her grandmother's hand. Hiralal too got off, playing his harmonium. Gohuman Bibi seemed to be looking for someone.

Shanichari walked hurriedly past Gohuman. She was scared of this woman.

You, little girl, Gohuman called out to her, Want a sweet?

No, no, I don't want anything.

Oh baba! She's a spitting cobra! Did Shanichari want to die of snakebite? Writhing in pain?

But as luck would have it, Gohuman smuggled out a few girls from their village that very same year.

That year too there was a drought. A drought meant no harvest. Coarse paddy, *gondli*, *maroa*, *sarguja*,[7] *uradh dal*[8]—nothing came up. The earth cracked. Even the forest floor did not yield a thing. No roots, no tubers.

It was at such a time that Gohuman Bibi landed up at the Banki village *haat*. She gathered all the girls under a tree. Treated them to *puris*[9] and *laddoos*. Then she said, Know of any girls who'll come to Kolkatta? Work there as *rejas* in the brick kilns?

The girls looked at each other.

See if you can find me some girls.

What kind of work?

My *malik* is like a god. Since I usually take village girls like you who've never been to a city, he first makes sure they get to look around a bit, see the sights, have some fun. Then he gives them work at his brick kiln.

Don't the local girls want to work as *rejas*?

The Kolkatta girls? They wear *chamak chamak*[10] saris, *chhamak chhamak*[11] jewellery, prance around the place. Their homes are overflowing with *puris* and *laddoos*. You think they'll work as *rejas*? Why should they?

Oh . . . !

You'll work four hours a day. Get 10 rupees a day. Don't have to worry about where to stay, what to eat, how to buy clothes. The *malik* will take care of everything.

We'll come.

No, no, hang on. Go home, talk it over with your parents. If they agree, only then will I take you. I don't go in for shady deals. I'm a local girl myself. I come from Lalpur, near the rail tracks.

The pangs of an empty stomach are hard to resist. If they worked in the brick kilns of Kolkatta they'd get enough to eat, wear dazzling clothes and see the sights of the city. The girls explained this to their parents that night.

Gohuman Bibi talked to their parents, gave each of them 50 rupees in advance, made them put their thumbprints on blank paper and took the girls away.

Those four girls from Shanichari's village never came back. The city did not return them. What could Gohuman Bibi do? Apparently the girls were busy making pots of money. They were prancing around in *chamak chamak* saris, anklets, bracelets and necklaces going *chhamak chhamak*. They hardly remembered Dhurbaha village with its cracked red earth and dilapidated huts. Those young girls, once someone's daughter, someone's sister, had been lured away by the city of Kolkatta.

Their mothers would sing while drawing water from the well,

I can hear the train whistling,
It took my girl away
To bake bricks in Kolkatta.

Meanwhile, the little brothers they had left behind grew up and were soon old enough to go coal-gathering near the railway tracks. The saplings they had seen when they left the village had flowered into fruit-bearing trees. Sometimes there would be a drought and the harvest would fail. At other times good rain would yield a rich crop. Slowly people began to forget those four girls. Who could remember forever those the city had taken away?

Mongru Oraon, too, never returned. Where was Kolkatta, where the brick kilns? Who could keep track of all this?

Shanichari came of age.

Shanichari was a big girl now. She was 16. Now she could go to the *haats* alone, both far and near. Her brothers were much younger. Shanichari was her parents' right hand. These days, like everybody else, she too took the *mahajan*'s grains to the *haat*. The *mahajan* owned a lot of land, had a large granary. Dhurbaha was a very remote village. She could make some profit if she went to the big and busy *haats*. She earned two rupees a day.

One day Shanichari stopped short at the *haat* in Rata. Hiralal! His hair had greyed and he was wearing glasses. But it was definitely Hiralal. Playing his harmonium and singing,

Lo aa gayi unki yaad
Woh nahi aye.[12]

Shanichari stood there for a minute.

Aren't you Moti Linda's daughter?

Yes. Recognize me?

You're from Chotti *tehsil*, aren't you?

Yes.

That grandmother of yours?

She's dead.

What do you do?

Sell the *mahajan*'s grain and pulses.

Good, good. Gohuman didn't get you?

No. Haven't seen her since then.

Oh, she'll be back. Last time, she took a few girls. Won't come for a few years. She's waiting for people to forget.

Then?

She'll lure new girls with promises of *chamak chamak* saris and *chhamak chhamak* jewellery.

Why don't the girls come back?

A monstrous city, Kolkatta. Devours everything around it—Ranchi–Singbhum–Palamau. Turns some girls into whores, sells off the rest.

Oh baba!

That's what Gohuman does with her deadly fangs.

Two years later, Shanichari voluntarily gave herself up to Gohuman's fangs. She was all set to get married to Chand Tirkey that year.

That was when the Adi Jati Raksha Morcha movement swept through the countryside. And why not? The winds of change and forest fires could sweep through jungles equally rapidly. The Raksha Morcha was fighting for the rights of the adivasis. But Dhurbaha village and its environs witnessed no such struggle. The Morcha called a big meeting at the Rata village *haat*. Many joined in with their bows and arrows. And why shouldn't they? After all the Morcha had promised them a new *azadi*.[13]

Sab julum bandh![14]

The forest is ours!

No more felling trees!

Parija Murmu had himself come to that meeting. And so had the police, lots of *meletary polis*.

Later, no one could tell if it was the police who fired first or Murmu who ordered his men to shoot their arrows. After all, these men went everywhere with their bows and arrows. So it was quite natural to bring them to the meeting. Some people were heard saying that the police opened fire when they saw that the men were armed. A few of the *meletary polis* were killed as well. And why wouldn't they be? Those who carry bows and arrows would obviously know how to use them.

All hell broke loose. People ran for cover to the primary health centre. The *meletary polis* entered the clinic firing. Later a *truk* was brought in to carry away the corpses.

Straight to the Mortongunj factory.

Quick! Throw the bodies into the furnace.

Take them away. Fast.

Eleven bodies. Only 11 to be left here.

Tell the Press. Official figure 11.

That's how a small place like Rata suddenly made the headlines. And the *meletary polis* was deployed in the region. Now there'd be no more newspaper reports. It was a question of prestige for the *meletary polis*. Don't try to stop us, *officer saab*, don't make us revolt.

Once we do that you'll lose all control.

Today the *pablic* condemns the Bihar *meletary polis*' misbehaviour. The moment the newspapers proclaim that the Bihar Military Police are 'revolutionaries', *pablic* opinion would immediately swing in their favour. Thanks to the Naxalite and the Jharkhand movements, a section of the *pablic* does have a soft spot for all 'revolutionaries'.

Don't stop us. Leave the area to us.

This is the first time their arrows have struck the BMP.

BMP kills, tribals die. This time things were different.

Don't try to stop us.

The officers said, Of course, of course, go ahead. We are BMP too. We want to be part of the action too. They got into the act as well.

A state and a central minister came to find out things firsthand after being continuously pestered by the media. But the BMP didn't let them in either.

Rata was now declared a protected area. The word *rata* meant 'red'. But BMP managed to turn red Rata into *ranka*. In other words, they stripped the place bare.

Which is why Shanichari felt the fangs of Gohuman.

You who have been reading this story must be wondering—so the Raksha Morcha *meeteng* set things ablaze, guns went bang bang bang, dark-skinned men and women screamed and ran helter skelter, the white walls of the health centre were stained red by the BMP who removed all but 11 corpses, and proclaimed this is a prestige issue, we'll set the forest on fire—but what does this have to do with Shanichari Linda, a lovely young Oraon girl, lush and lissom as the kusum tree?

You are also likely to think that this author is obsessed with issues like police–struggle–violence–adivasi–raksha morcha and so on. That nothing else interests her.

But look, there's basically just the one question. *Kaise bache*? How does one survive? Well, this writer chose her path long ago—that of writing such stories. Asking herself what to write about, she trudged mile after mile down innumerable roads which all led to one destination. At the end she always stood face to face with battles, blood, sweat, tears. That's why I decided to tell you Shanichari Linda's story.

The link between the Raksha Morcha meeting and Shanichari meeting Gohuman is both real and strong.

Did you ask why? Don't. You are intelligent, educated people. You know how such things work. Doesn't sugar cost you the earth because the sugar barons of north India pump a lot of money into donations, during elections? Even your morning cup of tea is intrinsically linked with the general elections in India.

Anyway, I'm not going to bore you with details of the sugar–coal–drugs nexus-plexus any further. Hats off to the government. It has hiked the price of essential commodities to help those who want higher profit margins, and made us realize that the saying *Dilli door ast*[15] is nothing but lies. Actually Delhi is just around the corner. From lighting the stove every morning to stirring sugar in your tea—it's Delhi all the way.

Let me tell you the inside story. I've seen Shanichari with my own eyes. And for the past one year, Janum Singh has been writing to me regularly from Rata. Of course, people like you don't want to believe in my kind of true stories. You've got so used to make-believe tales that true stories don't attract you any longer.

Who's to blame for all this? Who's responsible?

Listen to Shanichari's story.

Once the police and the BMP took over Rata and its adjoining areas, there was no stopping them. Janum Singh wrote, 'The BMP, CRPF and BSF[16] are *combing* the entire area and have unleashed a reign of terror. They are killing, torturing, plundering, destroying the crops in the field. It's inhuman. They've devoured all the poultry and goats. Smashed the ploughs. Destroyed whatever few possessions there were. Pots and pans, huts, all razed to the ground. The homeless adivasis have been driven to shelter in the forest. They have no rice, no salt. No clothes. They are hiding in the hills and forest caves. Families are split up, lost. No one knows where anyone is.'

You may have guessed by now that Janum Singh is a Bengali. I cannot disclose his identity. Besides, he's never wanted people to know who he is. You must be quite familiar with the long and lofty salutation to Sabyasachi in *Pather Dabi*.[17] I silently salute Janum Singh in a different kind of way. But this is not the time to wax lyrical about people like him. This is an hour of crisis. I just want you to know the meaning of his name. The word *janum* means 'thorn' in the Ho tongue. This Janum Singh is a thorn for some people and to some others he's *bah*—a flower.

Notice the phrase 'no clothes' in Janum's letter. Clothes—a whole new sari is a source of great empowerment. I know you'll realize this yourselves. How do I know this? Don't some of you buy saris worth thousands of rupees every Puja?

What else can I say? The reign of terror that was unleashed in Rata after the Raksha Morcha *meeteng* continued unabated, forcing the young women to flee to the forest. They didn't have any clothes. The BMP had burnt down their huts along with the saris—coarse, white, multicoloured—that they had bought from the *haat* with the little money they had managed to earn after hours of back-breaking labour.

The BMP took the young girls into the forest and raped them. Imagine the scene. Familiar to you, no doubt, from innumerable story books—the lush green forest and a group of Ho–Oraon–Munda girls who look as if they have been exquisitely carved out of black stone. Only the bestial howls of the BMP would have been left out of such a picture-book scene.

Without clothes, the girls are forced to hide in the forest. And it was at such a time that Gohuman Bibi appeared, like a veritable goddess. She told them, We'll get you new clothes and take you to Kolkatta to work in the brick kilns. You'll work hard, eat well, make money. Come, come! Scores of young girls were bitten by Gohuman's fangs. There isn't just the one Gohuman, after all, hundreds of similar snakes are slithering around, now that they sense an opportunity. And it's easy for them to gain entry to the area.

The local police got a cut. The GRP,[18] too, got their share.

Of course, I cannot disclose the identities of all those who were bribed by Gohuman to turn a blind eye and pretend, We saw nothing, we heard nothing. But I will not hesitate to state that if this last group of people had intervened, those girls could not have been smuggled out so easily.

Shanichari went with them.

Oh, did I not mention that Chand Tirkey was amongst those shot dead by the police at the Rata meeting, his body loaded onto a *truk* and carted off to be burnt in the furnace?

Shanichari had loved Chand. On the run from the BMP, she would remember Chand and realize that her emotions were burnt to ashes. Of course, everything may burn to cinders but the pangs of hunger refuse to die. The forest provided enough roots and tubers for them to survive on. But the forest could not provide them cloth to hide their shame.

Which is why Shanichari felt Gohuman's fangs. And in house after house, dark-skinned, grieving mothers sang,

My girl could live on tubers,
Wear leaves and buds in her ears,
Alas, trees can't grow clothes
And so my girl, said Ma-*go*,
To the brick kilns I must go
To the brick kilns I must go.

They took the night train to Howrah. From there, a bus ride to the Shyambazar five-point crossing. Then to Barasat, to Rahmat Sardar's 'Taraknath'-brand brick kiln. You must, of course, know how very little it costs to run a brick kiln and how very high the profits are. Which is why people like Rahmat, Irfan or Shiulal from north Bihar have opened these kilns in and around Kolkatta. They force the poor small farmers to give up their land by offering them money or by terrorizing them through local musclemen.

Thereafter the neighbouring farmer voluntarily sells off his land at a throwaway price. And why shouldn't he? His land becomes a public thoroughfare for the coolies and labourers working in the adjoining brick kiln. His crops are destroyed. So he sells off his land.

After all, people like you are busy building your houses—big houses, small houses, dream houses, foreign picture-book houses, matchbox flats, skyscraper office buildings and what not. Brick piled upon brick.

Due to the searing temperature of the furnace, the soil around a brick kiln becomes barren for a few hundred years. But that's none of your business. Let the paddy fields go. What have you got to do with paddy, after all? You're a rice eater.

Shanichari and the others reached Rahmat's brick kiln in mid-September. Yes, the kilns run from mid-September, just after the rains, to mid-June, the onset of the monsoons. Three months shut. Nine months open.

The wall surrounding the brick kiln was as high as a jail wall. Inside were Rahmat and his goons' pucca houses. Rahmat inspected all the girls thoroughly. Then he escorted them to Indrapuri.[19]

A row of pigsties. Walls of palm leaf thatched with coconut leaves. Shanichari's throat went dry at the sight. She asked for some water.

A single tubewell. One tubewell for 300 people.

Rahmat ordered, Out with your names. All of you bastards. You there, start.

Shanichari Linda. Father Moti Linda. Village Dhurbaha. P. S. Rata.[20]

You dumb idiot, have you written it down?

Yes, *huzoor*.

Read it out.

Somni Oraon. Father Kormu Oraon. Village Baheria. P. S. Lohardaga.

Well done. Listen, you bunch of animals. No one will ever be able to trace you here. So there's no point in trying to talk to anyone on the outside. You work, you get paid every week. No off-days. Now listen . . .

They listened.

After working here nine months you'll realize you were better off with the BMP.

Ai baba!

Hah! The *rejas* will carry the bricks, the *patariyas* will place them, the labourers will dig the ground and the *rubbishmen* will handle the kiln. Got it?

Huzoor.

You'll carry unbaked bricks in piles of 10. Each time, my *munshi*[21] will give you a *tikli*.[22] After you've carried 210 bricks and got 21 *tiklis*, you earn a rupee. Baked bricks will also be carried in piles of 10. After you've got 44 *tiklis* for 440 bricks, you'll make a rupee. Now go. Eat your *roti-sabji*[23] and go to sleep.

They looked at each other in shocked silence. Are they now prisoners in this alien land under these alien circumstances?

Go, go. Move.

They had begun to move. Suddenly Shanichari said, We won't work here. Send us back.

Indeed. And who'll pay your train fare?

Train fare? We travelled without tickets thanks to the bribe you paid the police.

Oh, ho! Quite a girl, this! Will you be able to find your way back home?

We'll ask people.

So you want to leave? Look there.

The gates were locked. The girls cried out in fright. Rahmat gestured to his men to drag the girls away. He grabbed Shanichari by the hand, saying, Come, share some meat curry and rice with me. You're just my type. Spunky girls like you are more fun.

Shanichari Linda's scream was cut off by Rahmat. His men continued pushing the other girls around.

Shanichari didn't find out what life was like as an ordinary *reja*. But her companions did. Joshima, Lugri, Jhini, Parai and Phulmani faced the worst. You work all day in the kiln. No matter how many bricks you actually carry, you get not more than 15 rupees a week. The rest of your earnings are deposited as *chapaiya* with the employer. To be given to you when you return home.

From that 15 rupees, you buy a week's ration of rice and salt. Eat rice or rice water mixed with salt and green chillies. Tea, *khaini*, oil, all come out of that money.

At the end of the day, when you're too tired to keep your eyes open, the head *mastaan* will call out your name in the daily auction. Today you go to him, tomorrow the driver, the day after the *munshi*.

You don't get holidays for the Pujas or for the festival of Holi. The owner doesn't care what the labour laws in Bihar or West Bengal are. Why should he, tell me? Why indeed? With the local police, mafia, in his pocket, he can't be bothered.

At home in the village, you are used to celebrating the spring with *Sarjombah*, welcoming the new leaves and budding flowers.

But here you're petrified of Holi. The *malik*'s friends arrive in hordes from Kolkatta. They force liquor down your throat till you pass out. Pull off your clothes. What happens next only your body knows.

Shanichari, of course, didn't have to pay such a heavy price. She belonged to Rahmat.

She would spit at the Gohumans when she saw them.

Gohuman would say, I was once a *reja* like you.

Thuu! *Thuu*! *Thuu*!

Now I do this kind of work.

You've turned into a snake.

How else would I survive?

Thuu! *Thuu*! *Thuu*!

Who's to blame for all this? Who?

Rahmat would dress Shanichari in good clothes and nice jewellery, rub fragrant oil in her hair—and then tear into her ruthlessly.

When Shanichari began throwing up one day, Rahmat said, From tomorrow you'll work as a *reja*. Josin will stay here with me. Lug bricks, get paid.

Lug bricks, lug bricks, Shanichari. You wonder where you are, where you've been brought—you can't quite figure out where this place is. With Rahmat's child in your womb, you stare blankly at the paddy fields stretching to the horizon. The endless fields beckon you to freedom, but you know you're a prisoner. You don't know the local language, nor do you remember the way here.

If you were carrying Chand Tirkey's child, your people would have accepted it. But how can you return home with a *diku*'s[24] child in your womb? In your mind's eye the paddy fields turn into the sal forest, the narrow path between the fields becomes an undulating hill track, and the quiet village in the distance turns into Dhurbaha.

Then one day the brick kiln shut down. Nobody got the *chapaiya* deposited with the employer. Rahmat handed a new *janta* sari[25] and a train *tikit* to each girl and sent them all home.

Shanichari too wore a new sari and, clutching a *tikit*, climbed on to the truck. All the other girls had also been abused, but she was the only one returning with a child in her womb. Gohuman had given the others pills.

When the train reached Chakradharpur, what a coincidence—Hiralal! Singing, *Lo aa gayi unki yaad*; and Shanichari burst into tears as soon as she heard him.

No, Shanichari Linda wasn't accepted in their village. What could they do? They lived their lives as victims of the *dikus*. How could their priest, the *naiga*, allow a woman carrying a *diku*'s child to be accepted in society?

Moti Linda, Shanichari's father said, I'll pay for a repentance feast.

Why should you? Is it Shanichari's fault? asked Chand Tirkey's elder brother.

That's the norm, said their *naiga*.

The repentance rites and the feast were held. Nevertheless, Shanichari remained an outcast. Her son was born. No, they didn't ask her to abandon the child. The Ho–Oraon–Munda–Santhals loved children.

Her parents asked, What will you do now?

You tell me.

Shanichari was unable to think clearly for a long time.

She would sit with her back to the wall and stare dully into the distance.

One day she bestirred herself. Sat up and said, Ma?

Yes?

Remember the four girls who never returned from the brick kiln?

Of course I do.

They were sold off.

Who sold them?

Malik.

Sold them?

Of course. They are sold off, turned into whores, made pregnant like me.

It's our destiny.

My son will never get married, Ma.

Why worry about that now?

Such boys can only get married to such girls. That's the *khawasin* custom.[26]

That's true.

How we despised them.

Don't think about it.

Don't want to. But I can't help it.

We're here for you, aren't we?

Ma, help me build a room for myself.

We will.

You look after the baby. I'll gather coal near the rail tracks and sell it.

He's still nursing.

I'll carry him on my back.

They put up a room for her. Walls of tree branches. Thatched with leaves. She cooked separately, ate alone.

Chand Tirkey's brother said, We should think about this as a community. There could be more Shanicharis in the future. Should we cast out our own women? Will that benefit our society?

The *naiga* said, We'll think about it if it happens again. Not now. This is a new problem.

Should the girls be allowed to go to the brick kilns?

Why not?

And after that?

I told you, we'll think about it later.

Shanichari didn't blame her people or ask any questions. She began collecting coal with her son strapped to her back. One day, after selling off the coal, she was buying some oil and salt. Suddenly she stopped short at the sight of Hiralal.

Hiralal!

Yes?

Why won't you look at me?

What will I see?

Shanichari smiled. Soothing him, she said, Gohuman Bibi too is not the real culprit. You didn't know that. But I've realized it.

Then who is, Shanichari? Who?

Everything around you, ev-er-y-thing. Shanichari stretched out her arms to include the world around her, standing stock still.

I know Shanichari is showing us who the real culprits are. I also know that she's waiting.

But I do not know how long she'll have to wait. Her story is not over. As long as people like Rahmat unabashedly run brick kilns, as long as Gohumans entice girls like Shanichari, till our motherland can provide basic food and clothing to girls like her, the freeze shot of Shanichari pointing her finger at the accused will remain.

The Fairytale of Rajabasha

THE HUSBAND'S NAME IS SARJOM PURTI, dear reader, and the wife's Josmina. Theirs was a true love marriage. Sarjom paid Josmina's father three cows as bride price and who else but Nandlal Shahu could lend him the money for that? Sarjom, euphoric in anticipation and lost in the dream of bringing home Josmina—bubbling and lively as the river Koyena in the monsoons—put his thumb impression on a blank sheet of paper. He took the money. Bought the cows from Jeeta Munda. They got married. The *dumang*[1] went *dham dham dham*. Music and dance, a grand feast for the kinsfolk. Rice and *kurthi dal*.[2] Sarjom's friends shot an arrow through the evil old wild boar with big tusks and solved the problem of fresh meat. Sura Jonko, who was much-travelled between Ranchi and Jamshedpur said, Not just turmeric and salt, let's cook it with onions, pepper and other spices.

Great fun, great food.

The two of them collected firewood and sold it at the *haat*. Worked hard breaking rocks and stones. And Nandlal never asked for his money.

They had a son. A lively child. The *tupuna mianba*[3] took place. The mother floated some rice in a basin of water and called out many names.

Budhu! Budhu!

The child screamed.

Mata! Mata!

The child screamed again.

Masidas! Masidas!

The child yawned and fell asleep. He was called Masidas. A very lively child.

Josmina was looking more beautiful than ever. Firm, statuesque body with sculpted lines, rough hair knotted in a large bun. Sarjom worked in Nandlal's field all day. He had to repay the loan. The Ho tribals of Kolhan[4] never left a debt unpaid. Who would want to be buried with an unsettled debt?

When people die, their funeral—*topajang*—takes place. The dead one is buried in the burial ground close to home.[5] On the seventh day, the door of his hut is kept open. The floor is covered with ash. The dead one is called by name throughout the night. Called by name every hour, with a handful of rice thrown outside the hut. In the morning, eyes bloodshot from staying up all night, the floor is checked for the footprints of a lesser animal.

If no such footprints are found, then the dead one has found a place among his ancestors, the *jiatatas*. If found, then the spirit of the dead has entered the body of the invisible animal for some reason. Perhaps because of an unpaid debt.

Which is why Sarjom, with his physique sturdy as a sarjom[6] or sal tree, laboured hard on Nandlal's land. At the end of the day he came home with a *paila* of *makai*.

Josmina collected roots and tubers from the forest. Living off just these and *ghato*[7] made of *makai*, she looked gorgeous. A new mother, the curves of Josmina's body filled out like the gushing Koyena in the months of rain. There was much happiness and peace in this first chapter of the fairytale of Rajabasha!

But the rains stopped one day. The clouds cast fleeting shadows on the *sabui* grass. The Koyena turned tame. The clear blue sky in the month of Bhaadro[8] made one long for something unknown. The autumn breeze made the forest restless.

In the next part of the tale there was starvation everywhere and people scavenged the forest for tubers and roots. They planted paddy on the *gora ote*, the dry land. But harvest time was still months away. In this chapter, a snake slithered into Sarjom's impoverished yet peaceful home through the crack caused by hunger. The snake was Nandlal Shahu.

He came wearing handstitched *nagras* of untanned leather which made a soft, squishy sound. Tossed some *khaini* into his mouth after rubbing it in the palm of his hand. His chest gleamed aggressively through his terrycot kurta. Pulling up his dhoti he scratched his thighs, and eyeing Josmina's bounteous breasts, muttered, Hai hai Ram!

Then he reminded himself of why he was here. In the month of September, Nandlal would tour the distant villages to find out about starving Kolhanis, Rautias, Harijans and Hos. He lived in nearby Chhotonagra, yet he had never done anything to help the starving people of Rajabasha. He had two fine houses in the districts of Monoharpur and Raikera. And two wives in those two houses. Now his first wife, who lived in Rajabasha, was pestering him for a pucca brick house.

What! They get to live in tall double-storeyed pucca houses painted deep blue! And for me a hut? They flaunt plastic flower vases with plastic flowers in them—and I'm to keep painting flowers and leaves on my walls? For them movies in Ranchi's cinema halls, for me a recital of Tulsidas's Ramayana, that too once a year! To hell with this household of *makai–kurthi*–cows–buffaloes–butter-milk and *gur*! I refuse to wait upon your mother, aunt and uncle wearing these cheap Bombay-mill saris with Vrindavani prints! I want to wear nylon saris and listen to the transistor! My skin is still so silky-smooth, even a fly can't get a foothold! My complexion is as golden as pure *ghee*. In what way am I less than them?

So this time Nandlal decided to visit Rajabasha. In this part of the fairytale one has to look for the story within the story. In August, Nandlal hotfooted it to Ranchi. Met Officer Sardar Malkhan Singh who gave him 20,000 rupees in cash on the spot.

Send the *maal*[9] to Punjab—100, all handpicked—and you'll get the rest of your dues—20,000 more in cash. I'll see to it that you make 40,000 a year. But make sure the goods are fresh and sturdy, so that my money doesn't go down the drain.

In search of the necessary *maal*, Nandlal had to return from Ranchi to Rajabasha. To Sarjom's hut.

What's wrong, babu?

Where's Sarjom?

Isn't he working on your field?

Yes, yes, that's right.

Then?

Something I want.

That loan?

No, not money.

But you're getting it back anyway. He's paying you back by working for you. And haven't you amassed a mountain of chiranji,[10] mahua and sal seeds from us in these three years? All for free. That too amounts to money. We need just five more *pailis* of sal seeds to square our dues. That's it.

And who's keeping these accounts?

Sura Jonko.

Sura Jonko!

Yes, babu.

So Sura Jonko's a big *leedar* now! Knows how to read and write. Incites all of you to go and claim the forest land. Well, since he's kept the accounts, I'll accept it. I live here, I have to trust you folks. I won't dispute his calculations. But still, it's not quite right.

Sura says you buy 10 *pailis* of sal seeds for five seers[11] of salt and sell it for 10 rupees. Buy one *paili* of chiranji for 15 rupees and sell it for 50 rupees. That's how you make your profit. You've taken maunds[12] and maunds from us, that's fine, but don't tell me the loan of 300 rupees is still not settled?

Okay, okay, it's settled.

Else Sura will go and settle accounts.

No, no, he doesn't have to. Anyway, I came to give you some news. There's a good job going. You'll both make good money, eat well. Ask Sarjom to see me. I'll give him the details.

All right.

Is Sura related to you in some way?

He's like family.

How come?

You won't understand, babu.

Perhaps. Ah, what a lovely little boy! With such a boy you ought to be looking forward to better days! If it wasn't for this loan . . . This is the time for you to be happy.

At this juncture of the fairytale of Rajabasha, Josmina stands astounded. The serpent that had slithered into their peaceful life, their poor but happy home, was actually saying, How miserable you are!

If you realize how hard it is for us, babu, why did you take mountain-loads of chiranji, mohua and sal seeds from us, worth so much money? Why do you make my man work free for you? You cause us all this misery and then you turn around and say 'How miserable you are!' Our only worry is paying you back. We have no other worries. With Masidas' father around, why should we be miserable?

That's true, that's true.

Nandlal went on his way.

Sarjom heard of this visit and went to see Nandlal.

What job were you talking about, babu?

An excellent job. Big farmers. Plenty to eat. Work for a short period. The two of you will get, say, about 400 a month. Enough clothes. Work for a year and at the end of it—*baap re baap*! You'll come back with almost 5,000 bucks! Sit at home and enjoy!

Let me ask Sura!

And where is he?

Who knows. Getting ready to fight for the right to the forest.

Who knows when he'll be back. If you wait to talk to him, Sarjom, it'll be too late.

Where's the place, babu?

You'll have to take a train.

Where?

Punjab.

How far?

How far is Ranchi?

A few hours away.

It's the same.

Sarjom thought it over for a while. Then he said, Let me go home. Discuss it with the mother of my son.

And discuss it they did. No, no, your babu is not a good man. Don't trust him. Let's not leave. Let's stick it out here. The Kolhan people have always starved till the spring harvest.

Then let me go.

And what about me?

They stared at each other. How could Sarjom leave her behind? He had got into debt just to be close to her. How could he leave her? The two of them would have to go together.

It would have been good if Sura was around. But where's he? Who knows. Come, Josmina, let's go. We'll take the train and reach in a jiffy. Earn pots of money. Then come back here and dig a well. This land won't be dry once it gets water. It'll turn fertile.

Josmina said, Let's go then. But how far away it seems!

Can't leave you behind.

Nandlal knew they would agree. He said, Leave everything to me. Everyone will want to go once they hear about this. Don't open your mouth to anyone. We have to go to Monoharpur first.

No, they didn't utter a word. This part of the fairytale is very confusing. They left very early in the morning. Walked 25 or 30 miles to Monoharpur. Reached in the late afternoon. Rested in a tin-roofed railway warehouse where they slept beside innumerable Sarjoms and Josminas.

Then they took the train to Tatanagar. The next day they boarded the Amritsar Mail.

Nandlal told the GRP, No profit in supplying coolies these days. You take a cut, so does the police.

Want it all, do you?

What to do! I'm growing old! Nowadays I just feel like relaxing at home. But is that possible?

Why, aren't you selling chiranji worth 20,000 rupees a year?

Hai Ram! Why don't people let these *junglees*[13] retain their innocence? That so-and-so Sura Jonko is a real bastard. He has raised a hue and cry that if the government does not purchase chiranji, mohua and sal seeds, the traders will have to pay the government rate.

Nandlal fed all of them *puris*, *kachauris*, *laddoos* and pickles on the train. And one must admit that though they ate to their hearts' content, Nandlal didn't grudge it at all. It's not a joke to feed 30 or 40 people on such a scale. Nandlal had very little to eat and dozed all the way. He muttered to himself from time to time. A 100 or 150 coolies to be supplied! How many trips will he have to make back and forth?

Nandlal Shahu/son of Girdhar Shahu/Village Chhotonagra. According to an unwritten contract, Nandlal would get a 100 to 150 per coolie supplied. The *maliks* in Punjab will pay. Malkhan Singh is the chief contractor. He will get 200 to 300 rupees per coolie. Nandlal is a sub-contractor. So who says he's getting too much?

He has to face all the trouble, put in the hard work. While you, Malkhan Singh, an officer in the Heavy Engineering Works, make money without as much as lifting a finger. You are the number one contractor of the Punjab *maliks*. And as for you, *malik*! How much are you actually making? How come you're willing to pay so much? Why not? The government minimum wage for harvesting wheat is Rs 17.55. Local farmhands get Rs 10.60. For coolies from other states it's Rs 10.08. But you don't pay even that. You'll put them on a monthly wage, cheat them even of that. Well-endowed, attractive women like Josmina are an added bonus.

The government rate for threshing wheat is Rs 13. The local labour takes Rs 11.33; for other coolies the rate is Rs 11.12. Of course, you never give them that. They are hired on monthly wages and you cheat them of that too. You're saving all the time. Thousands and thousands of rupees. Dark-skinned, firm-fleshed Josminas are an added bonus.

The minimum wage for sowing, harvesting and threshing paddy is Rs 10.30. The local hands get Rs 8.69 but for coolies from other states the rate is Rs 8.20. You, of course, never pay that. You hire them on monthly wages and again cheat them of that. You're saving a lot. The terrified looks and helpless pleas—'no . . . no . . . no'—of women like Josmina are an added bonus.

You're saving thousands. '*Punjab ka kisan, adarsh kisan*!'[14] The investment behind the prosperity of the *maliks*, Malkhans and Nandlals are these dark-skinned people. Long live the Alagkhand movement.[15] Today these dark-skinned *junglees* fight for their rights with bows and arrows. The next day the police and the military chase them. They uproot these aboriginal people both from the forest and from their land. On which they settle traders, contractors and officers from north Bihar. This is what the government's five-pronged resettlement *prograam* in the forest areas is all about.

Nandlal rubbed some *khaini* on his palm.

There is no real end to a fairytale.

In the next part of the tale they reached Punjab, and Nandlal found the *maliks* at the station. No, Gurubhajan Singh was not there. Never mind. Niranjan Singh from Haripur village of Ferozepur district gave Josmina a keen once-over and pinched Sarjom's arm and shoulder muscles.

Nandlal sold them both for 400 rupees.

From the station to *malik*'s village in a jeep. Village? Towns would be put to shame. Sarjom and Josmina were awed by the terry-nylon clad Niranjan, with his massive wristwatch and his nylon turban. The child began to cry and Josmina, gaping open-mouthed at everything around her, put a nipple to the child's mouth. Niranjan shut his eyes. Feed her for a week and these goods will be just right. Milk, *rotis*, vegetables.

Niranjan's house was single-storeyed, spic and span, spread over at least 10 *kathas*[16] of land. A huge barn stood in the yard, surrounded by a wall. He had an electric irrigation pump, a tractor. A washing machine at home. This and other gadgets were all *phorrain*. His wife, a nylon-clad disgruntled looking Sardarni, took one look at them and went inside.

Niranjan's man-Friday Harchand took them to a tiny room. Brought them *roti*, *dal* and *sabji*. That's the shit-house, and there's the tap. Don't mess up the place, you *junglee jaanwars*[17] from Bihar.

The *malik* sent for them in the late afternoon.

Sarjom, you will get 80 rupees a month; plus food, clothes and a railway ticket. Your job is to take care of the cows and buffaloes from four to eight in the morning. After that you work in the fields, irrigate the sugarcane and wheat fields, and do whatever else is required.

But *malik*! Nandlal Shahu told us something else.

What did he say? You *junglee* swine from Singbhum! What did Nandlal say?

He said, '. . . you'll get 100 rupees per head, per month.'

That's what it comes to. I'll be spending at least a hundred rupees on the wheat, rice and *sabji* you eat.

But . . .

One word more and I'll chop you into pieces and bury you in the wheat field. Turn you into fertilizer . . . ha ha ha!

I won't work.

No? Your father will work! Your grandfather will work! I bought you and your wife from Nandlal for 400 bucks.

Hai Hai Josmina!

Yes! This Josmina will sweep the cowshed, courtyard, kitchen and house. Then she'll work in the sugarcane field.

Thus did one of Punjab's *adarsh kisans* set them a daily routine of 16 to 18 hours' labour. This farmer's con-tri-bution to the nation's agro-economy was significant. Virbhumi Punjab![18] From military service to the hotel trade, from the truck business to garage service, from government civil servants to contractors in Bihar—who could stop Punjab?

Niranjan patted Josmina on the arm and said, You'll get 40 rupees a month.

Sarjom said, Josmina! He wants you.

I won't let him touch me.

They spoke in hushed tones, in whispers. Once they had entered their cell-like room in the barn, Harchand locked the door from outside. It was his job to keep the buffaloes, cows and bonded labour under lock and key.

Both of them felt totally crushed.

Listen, can't we escape?

How, Josmina?

By which route did he bring us? Where are we?

I can't figure it out, Josmina.

Listen, they speak Hindi here!

Yes, Josmina, now I know that they have been bringing us here for years. That's why even though they don't understand our language, they get by with Hindi.

Listen, I don't feel good about the place at all!

Josmina! Don't frighten me, please! And be careful.

Listen, will he send me to the same field as you?

Who knows! Look! No use worrying. Let's dance to their tune for a while. At the first opportunity, we'll escape. Let me get a hang of the roads.

Next morning, Harchand gave Sarjom navy-blue jeans and a matching T-shirt. Sardarni, the sardar's wife, gave Josmina a salwar-kameez. Wear this. Take off your dirty rags. Put the child down and go to work. There shouldn't be a speck of dirt anywhere. Take the broom, get started.

After cleaning the house, Josmina washed four buckets of clothes. Why use the *phorrain* washing machine if cheap labour is in abundant supply. Niranjan said, Look! So many kinds of soap and so many brooms! We have an efficient system.

At 11, Josmina ate a bowl of *dalia* made of crushed wheat, took her baby and went into the sugarcane field. In a piece of rag, she tied up her midday meal of *roti* and *sabji*. Niranjan said, We give *rotis* plus vegetables. We have an efficient system.

Josmina carried her son on her hip. She felt safe when her son was with her. She saw a small hut in the middle of the sugarcane field. Harchand told her, You can have your lunch in that room. Put your son to sleep there and get to work.

She looked around but couldn't see Sarjom. Some women and men were working in the sugarcane fields. They were locals. They spoke to her in a Hindi she could follow and asked what had happened to the labourers from the previous year. Josmina knew nothing about them. Surinder, a strongly built middle-aged woman, said, Your husband has been put to work somewhere else. This *malik* is a real bastard!

Then she said, He doesn't want to employ us. We have to be paid 10 rupees a day. You people are really unfortunate to fall into the clutches of such a scoundrel! Listen, don't step into that hut. The *malik* uses it for all sorts of wickedness.

A few days later, the *malik* came to the hut and stripped Josmina naked. Baby Masidas watched in fear as his mother was abused. Arrey, this hut is here just for this—ha ha ha. We have an efficient system. Come on, put on your clothes. Seen how virile I am?

At night Josmina turned her face away, lay like a stone. Sarjom, with all his manhood and deep love for Josmina, lay dumb, enraged by the futility and helplessness of the protest smouldering within.

Then Josmina said dryly, He'll do it every day.

Don't say that!

You ask around. The locals will tell you how to escape. They don't want us to work here. They know that the *malik*'s a bastard.

Yes, I will.

Ask them.

I will.

Sarjom drew Josmina close to him. Ran his fingers tenderly all over her body and said, I don't blame you. This is our fate!

Was the village deity offered a puja?

When?

When we got married?

Yes! Of course!

Then how could this happen?

We were starving at home.

But why? Sura had said Kolhan would give us enough to eat.

Perhaps, someday.

Will you leave me?

No, Josmina!

Everyone's out to cheat us! Rob us. Nandlal gives us salt in exchange for sal seeds, mohua and chiranji! Cheats!

Yes, Josmina. They're all cheats!

Niranjan Singh came the next day and the next. Gradually, Josmina turned into a ghost-ridden presence. She would get up at four in the morning and put on the salwar-kameez. Then she would sweep the cowshed, the courtyard and the house. Wash all the clothes and leave for the sugarcane fields. At *tiphin time* she would surrender her body to Niranjan and work in the fields again. When she got back, she would sweep the room and the cowshed and work like a machine till eight at night.

She no longer said, Come on, let's leave.

This is how she turned into a robot controlled by Niranjan. A slow fire smouldered in Sarjom's head. He went about his work with a frowning, tight-lipped face.

One day Sukhram told him, Leave this place!

Go where?

Do you want to?

Right away.

I'll show you the way.

Show me.

You may not get your dues.

Never mind!

But Josmina said, How can we leave?

We'll escape.

Josmina patted her abdomen.

What about the seed the *malik* has sown here? Shall I take it with me?

Oh Josmina! Sarjom moaned like a wounded animal whose throat had been pierced with an arrow so its cry could not be heard. Josmina stared at him, confounded. Then she said, You go.

Where?

Home.

And you?

Take our son with you.

And you?

How can I go? If I bear a *diku*'s child they'll make us outcasts. Forget me. Get married again.

I won't leave you behind.

Won't you?

It's not your fault!

At this point in the fairytale, Niranjan took charge of their lives. Because Josmina told him, Let Sarjom leave.

What? You mean you prefer me? Ha ha ha.

Josmina stared at him, astonished. The more she saw of Niranjan, the more stupified she grew. To Niranjan she was just fresh meat; dark, *junglee* flesh which he had paid for. They bought it all up, everything. Everything that belonged to the Josminas.

No, I don't.

Then?

I'm pregnant.

My child?

Yes.

How can you be sure?

Sarjom doesn't sleep with me any more.

Why?

Once a *diku* touches me, I can't sleep with him. That's the norm.

If Sarjom goes, what about you?

That's your problem.

Niranjan got worried. He took Josmina into town, aborted the foetus, brought her back. Josmina lay limp, exhausted. She had been let off work. For three days. Sarjom told her, Let's escape now.

Where to?

Let's see.

He told Harchand, Don't lock the door at night. Josmina needs to get up several times.

They escaped at night. Left behind four months' dues with Niranjan. Scaling the boundary wall they ran to Sukhram's house, where they rested that night. Started walking the next night. They reached Karnal Singh's house in Johan village. Budha Purti of Chhotonagra village was supposed to be there.

But Budha wasn't. Karnal Singh had sold him. It was a big mistake to have bought him for 200 rupees in the first place. He could barely work 16 hours a day without wheezing and panting. So, you've run away from Niranjan Singh. Good, very good. That man is no good, you know. Brags about his *phorrain* washing machine. Huh! I own a *phorrain* washing machine *and* cooking range.

Sarjom got a grey pair of jeans and a green T-shirt and Josmina got a salwar-kameez. The same work-routine, the same everything. This time they were not locked up at night and Karnal Singh took Josmina away at nine every evening.

Why shouldn't I? Did Niranjan spare you, you wild *junglee* female? Don't pretend to be so virginal!

Sarjom slept with his son.

They ran away after a month. Another Sukhram helped them. They were caught by Pritam Singh of Kosa village. Yes, yes, you're runaway coolies, aren't you? I'll hand you over to the police. There's no one to help you.

The local labourers were friendly. Told them, Go on, run!

And why wouldn't they encourage you? They lose their jobs to you lot.

Sarjom said, Fine! We'll work for you. But you can't touch my wife.

Of course not, your wife's like a mother, a sister, to me.

But after a few days Pritam started sending for the mother-and-sister-like Josmina.

So they ran away.

No money, nothing at all, Josmina! How do we go home? We've come to Sardar Gyan Singh of Hoshiarpur. He'll give me 100 and you 50! We have to earn some money for the train fare!

We had no choice but to come here. Couldn't walk any more, I was so weak, Josmina. I was running a fever at Pritam Singh's house. You stroked my limbs so tenderly, massaged my head so caringly that the *malik* started to send for you. So we had to run away.

Sarjom kept talking like this all the time. Sometimes to Josmina, at other times to himself. Talked while watering the sugarcane field. The sugarcane plants nodded in assent. He told them what he couldn't tell Josmina.

Josmina would go to sleep listening to him. Suddenly she said, Listen! I've thought of something.

Tell me!

Are we suffering so much because we named the boy Masidas? Listen, pay attention. My mother had told me not to!

Something seemed to have come undone in Sarjom's brain. He asked helplessly, Why should the name Masidas cause such misfortune?

That's a good one! We aren't Christians, are we? Why name him Masidas?

But you gave him the name!

And you never objected. When others did, you told them, What's in a name?

Yes, so I did. So what? If we've offended the gods with this name, I'll offer a puja and make amends. When they make us *jatietka*, outcasts, we can offer puja, feed *jatimardi*, the village society, and absolve ourselves of all our sins. Isn't that so?

No, not always.

Not always?

Josmina shook her head and, resting it on Sarjom's shoulders, stared into the darkness. Then, very slowly, she told Sarjom another episode of this fairytale.

No, not always, dear. If a woman returns home pregnant with an outsider—a *diku* child—there is no forgiveness. The village society imposes *jatietka* on them. Even if they offer puja, even if they hold a feast or *jatimardi*, they can't get *jatirakab*—get accepted. They have to build their huts at a distance from the rest, and after they die, they are buried elsewhere, not in the family burial ground.

Please press my head a little. So many worries. It feels like my head's going to burst.

Not all sins are forgiven! How did Chhotonagra get its name? Once upon a time, deep in the forest lay two magical *nagaras*, two drums of cast iron! Didn't catch rust, didn't age or weather. People say that after Tatanagar was founded, the *dikus* started making steel. But so many moons ago, there were no *dikus*. And the people of Kolhan made those *nagaras* then.

Stroke my hair, will you?

The twin *nagaras* lay in the forest. Then someone took one to Monoharpur and built a temple. Even now the Raja of Monoharpur . . . how poor he is . . . he even asks us for paddy . . . the Raja worships the *nagara* on Dussera. We send a goat as an offering. After the sacrifice, the Raja gets the head and we get the rest of the meat. And we all dance together, all the adivasi peoples!

Please go on. Your words flow like the river Koyena, it soothes me.

The *dikus* took that *nagara* and built a temple. Raised a wall around the *nagara* of Chhotonagra. But the twin *nagaras* should have stayed in the forest. There was a time when we would beat the *nagaras* when the enemy entered Kolhan. How far the drumbeats travelled! It would say, Children of Kolhan! Beware! Beware!

Please massage my chest, Josmina. It's burning. My chest . . . oh!

But we forgot to beat the *nagara* when the likes of Nandlal entered! When was the *nagara* beaten? When a girl gave birth to a *diku* child! Society made such a girl *jatietka*! Now the *nagara* is never beaten. But the mother is made a *jatietka* if she bears a *diku*'s child. Kolhan does not know how to forgive.

I can't live without you.

Get some sleep!

And you?

I'll sleep too.

Josmina knew that Kolhan would not forgive her. She strokes him with loving fingers. Sarjom was like the blood in her veins. But Kolhan was so unforgiving! The *diku* robs the children of Kolhan of their religion, language, music, dance, land, forest and minerals. Kolhan can't do a thing. But if a *diku* plants a seed in a daughter of Kolhan, the seed is poison. Burn the soil, sacrifice the girl.

Kolhan won't forgive her. The *malik* won't leave her alone. Josmina shut her eyes.

There was nothing *phorrain* about Gyan Singh. He was every inch an Indian. Dragging Josmina away, he poured liquor down her throat and told his cohorts, You can have her, one by one.

Sarjom remained locked in the room.

After four months Sarjom said, I have to send money home. Give me my dues.

Gyan Singh gave him 400 rupees.

What about the rest—200?

Later.

Sarjom and Josmina ran away that night, with the help of yet another Sukhram. How exhausting and repetitive a part of their life story all this running away is! But then again, it's the truth, and for that very reason, a fairytale. For fairytales are stories which have a beginning but no end.

In the next episode, they are given shelter by Sardar Sarban Singh of Badala village of Kapurthala district.

Sarban Singh alarms them and they wake as if from a spell, writhing in unbearable pain. What on earth is going on? What's happening?

Because Sarban put them on the same work schedule. But gave the three of them plenty to eat. Milk, *roti*, *dal* and vegetables. They were allotted a good room. Sarban Singh lived alone. His son lived in town. A widower, Sarban retired to bed at nine. He told Sarjom, Keep your door locked. Don't open, even if someone knocks.

What's this? They had never seen a *malik* like him. Josmina and Sarjom were terribly scared. This couldn't be real! It must be a dream!

Then after a month, normalcy was restored. Because Sarban's son, the young sardar Dileep Singh, a '*phorrain*-returned' contractor, sauntered to the sugarcane field, grabbed Josmina and got into the act.

It went on for a long, very long time, his performance and his gratification.

The next day Josmina and Sarjom went to Sarban. Hanging his head in shame, Sarban gave them a full month's pay. My truck's leaving now. It will take you to the station.

The station. Then Tata, Monoharpur and eventually Rajabasha.

The hut had to be raised anew. It had to be freshly plastered with cow dung and clay. It was the month of September once again. The lean season. Need to buy some baskets from the *mahalis*,[19] to collect firewood from the forest. We've some money left. Let's buy two goats. They'll graze, give birth to more. And listen, we must change Masidas' name.

Within no time everything became as it was before. It was so refreshing to bathe in the waters of the Koyena. So peaceful to boil some *makai* at the end of the day and cook *ghato* in the evening. To sprinkle salt on it and eat off leaf plates. So pleasant to sit by the banks of the river, washing pots and pans while chatting to girls you've known all your life.

Did you observe *Sarjombah* this year?

There are no sarjom–sal trees there. But I had my Sarjom with me.

Well said!

He's my Sarjom, and I am his *bah*, his flower.

Give her a good splashing! You've learned to talk so cleverly!

No, no, I couldn't bring anything back with me. And listen, if Nandlal or his kind ever entice you to go, don't listen to them. Don't go. It's hell out there. The *maliks* are all beasts.

Two months passed this way. Masidas' name was changed to Mata. Such peace, such happiness! Josmina had bought two goats. She guarded them zealously. Every evening she tethered them inside the hut.

Gradually it was getting colder, the days growing shorter. By late afternoon the long shadows of the hills flowed down silent as water to envelop the whole village. And in the forest, the trees shed their leaves. It's time to harvest the spring crop. The time has come.

Then, on a perfectly happy and peaceful day, Josmina, while reaping paddy, suddenly heard *dhim*! *dhim*! *dhim*! The sound of the iron *nagara* coming from afar, from beyond the foothills, and Chhotonagra and the forests.

She sprang up and looked around her in terror. No, they were reaping paddy on the slope of the hill. The same clear cloudless sky, with birds circling over the fields. The boys were rattling tin drums to chase away the birds. No one had heard it.

But she continued to hear that sound. Like someone driven by spirits, she threw down the sickle and started walking briskly. Then she began to run, clapping her hands over her ears. Reaching a distant, lonely spot, she fell face down on the ground. The *nagaras* were splitting her ear drums. The ancient Kolhan was warning Josmina.

Josmina vomited.

Then she went down to the river. Taking off her clothes, she bathed. She thought it over. No, it was not Sarjom's child. No bleeding for two months. Two months ago that young sardar . . . in the sugarcane field . . . Josmina had thought everything would turn out all right . . . but it did not . . . now this vomiting . . . familiar symptoms . . . yes, it all added up.

Should she tell Sarjom?

Jatietka, jatietka!

Sarjom would go mad. Run from door to door. Plead with the community, I'll sell the goats, give you money, do whatever penance you prescribe. But please don't make us outcasts.

And Sarjom too will be made an outcast!

A hut outside the village, a burial place marked for outcasts. No one willing to give their daughter to Mata when it came time for him to marry. They'd be ostracized during *Sarjombah*.

Sarjom, Sarjom! In the fairtytale of Rajabasha you are my sal tree and I am your flower. But a thunderstorm swept me away and threw me to the ground. The fairytale of Rajabasha is the fairytale of Kolhan too. The fairytale of Kolhan is its very history. Oh waters of the Koyena, flow on, flow on. Josmina will come to you to tell her tale.

She returned home. Plastered the freshly-plastered hut. Drove the goats indoors. Fetched Mata home from her mother's, then cooked some rice. There was still a little rice left.

When Sarjom returned, Josmina served him with tender care. Then lulled him to sleep, lovingly caressing his body, his hair.

When she got up, when she left home, Sarjom had no idea.

Josmina went to the river Koyena. She took off her sari, her cheap brass bangles, her chain and ear studs, and placed them on a rock. Sarjom would bury all these with her. She entered the water, stayed afloat, then dove down deep clasping a rock under water. Oh Koyena, please ask Kolhan not to make Sarjom pay a penance. He doesn't have money. He only has twice 20 rupees left. How can he pay?

Koyena heard everything and conveyed her message to Kolhan. Then, at one point, Kolhan drew Josmina deep into her lap.

Not early morning, they found Josmina in the late afternoon. Yesterday, she was seen vomiting while reaping paddy. Today, Josmina's nude body looked innocent and pure, washed by the waters of a calm river! They all looked at one another. Sarjom covered Josmina's nudity. Lifted her in his arms. Rubbing his face in her hair he said, You will sleep in our courtyard, yes, at home. You are innocent.

The people built a *machan*, all of them came forward. Could Sarjom carry her alone? Rajabasha was quite a distance away!

The wind blew, the Koyena flowed on, the fairytale of Rajabasha did not end, not all fairytales do . . .

Only, at the end of this episode, Josmina, after snuffing out her dreams, slumbers on.

Chinta

EVERY YEAR A GROUP OF PEOPLE from the Danton and Contai region in Medinipur migrated to Calcutta.

Medinipur should have been able to provide them not only with a place to live but with the means to live as well. But areas like Danton, Ghatal or Kanthi are hardly ever able to do that. Therefore, every year at the onset of the monsoons or after the autumn harvest, these people would arrive. Their very appearance reeked of the village. Men like Ananta–Utsab–Chaitanya–Akrur—Shahus, Pradhans or Mahants—would first hang around their fellow villagers, the fitters and plumbers of Calcutta Corporation. Some of the newcomers would turn up in our neighbourhood to replace cooks like Kailash or Ananta who were heading home for a while. Descendants of quite a few middle-class Bengali families, Ghosh–Bose–Sircar–Chatterjees, who had originally acquired some swampland in the city when it was going dirt cheap, could still afford to retain these full-time cooks. Thanks to their inheritance of a couple of houses or some arable land in places like Canning, they still didn't have to worry about two square meals of coarse rice and a fish like *tangra* cooked in a thin gravy every day. That's what made these families stay together even today. Such households usually ran a joint kitchen. Despite living under the same roof, each unit of the larger family kept its own separate stash of things—the best apples or cheap sweetmeats—according to the incomes of the male earning members. Cooks like Ananta or Kailash usually found jobs in households like these. They would boil rice, cook the daily fish curry, occasionally make spicy fish dishes for expectant mothers. They would argue at times with the mistress of the house over their monthly allowance of soap and washing powder, paan and *supari*.[1] In the afternoons, they would gather on the porch and hold court amidst the newcomers from Medinipur.

Their women would usually form groups and rent rooms in the slums. They would take jobs as part-time maids who went from house to house; sometimes they also worked as live-in maids.

I had first seen Chinta amongst these women. Short, fair, wearing silver bangles and a tattooed necklace. She was working at my neighbours' while her little girl sat with a rope tied around her waist. The mistress of the house was rather fastidious about cleanliness. She wouldn't tolerate a skinny, two-year-old girl running after her mother from room to room. I too found her intolerable at first. What an emaciated child! Just sitting there in the dust of the porch. A sickly face which made her look really ancient. Huge vacant eyes, with no trace of a child's curiosity. She sat there with an air of great fatigue, patience and forgiveness. The neighbourhood children stood close by watching her. Their little faces animated with a beastly curiosity and a cruel urge to prod the weak. Of course, one couldn't blame them!

Their families virtually survived on the meagre rent collected from tenanted properties. They had never known an affectionate, cordial atmosphere. The curse of the joint family is that members usually hate one another fiercely. Children suffer as a result, bearing the cross of such superficial relationships. Having never enjoyed a childhood, growing up in an atmosphere of dead relationships, they age fast.

Chinta's daughter and the reaction she provoked among the other children, gave me a jolt. The hollowness of the system I lived in suddenly dawned on me. I was ashamed and this made me rather merciless. That was the best form of defence, after all! I said, Why have you kept her tied up? Isn't it hurting her?

I have work to do, she said and looked at me with the eyes of a cowed animal. She washed huge piles of dishes and ground vast quantities of spices. Late afternoon I would see her returning home with the girl in her arms. As she walked back slowly, her damp clothes attracting the leering glance of the paanwalla, one could make out that she was soon to bring forth another child as playmate to the already malnourished one in her arms. Later, I couldn't resist asking her, Don't you have anyone at home? Can't you leave your daughter with them?

I have no one.

She had no one. That she had to fend single-handed for her daughter, her unborn child and herself was obvious when, on cold winter mornings she took a bath and went to work in her faded and threadbare sari, when she managed to somehow put down a mid-morning meal of left-over rice, sitting next to her daughter on the veranda or when she had to run around at the end of the month for her wages of eight rupees. Fully aware of how helpless she was, the mistress of the house where she worked had vociferously bargained for a salary of eight rupees a month when the going rate was 12. But she was always as patient and uncomplaining as a beast of burden. Sometimes, she didn't even get her full pay. She would say, I had to pay a *phine.* Sometimes, I haven't been given a sari. I felt embarrassed by her condition and placated my middle-class conscience by giving her an old sari or handing a few titbits to her daughter. When she left late at night after a day's work, the paanwalla—not drunk, fully in his senses—tried to clasp her in his arms. In the process, tearing her sari. He laughed and began to sing out loud. Next morning, the landlady's pet crow, sporting an ornamental nose-ring, snatched a biscuit from the little girl's grasp. Even the crow knew that the child was helpless and had a rope tied to her waist. Thus my patchy attempts to pacify a guilty conscience proved futile: such attempts come to nought in this world.

Meanwhile, Chinta had another daughter. The other women who had come with her to the city had already managed to save up a bit. I got the news from them. Of late, she had even lost the job that had paid her eight rupees a month. I realized from the other maids' chatter that Chinta was going through really hard times. She had had to pawn her silver bangles for 10 rupees. I also realized that her fellowmates were keen to lend her a little money in exchange for her utensils. They said, She has some fine bell metal bowls and glasses. It's unlikely that she'll ever be able to claim them back. I realized that this was just another opportunity for exploitation.

In a few days she was back at work, still unsteady and terribly weak. Told me, I've left the elder one with the younger child this time, Ma. Poor people like us are killed off in many ways. Of course, I didn't need to learn this from Chinta. I had always prided myself on being a friend of the underprivileged. Such feelings of self-gratification were not always subconscious! Possibly I was impelled to do something to improve her situation. Perhaps this philanthropic trait was part of my middle-class inheritance—a class which thought a great deal about being benevolent to others at no cost to themselves. Such values were indeed rooted in decadence. Therefore, my efforts at giving old, torn clothes, stale bread or an extra orange to Chinta, made not an iota of difference to her misfortune. It was as meaningless as trying to conceal a crack in a grimy wall by putting up a pretty *calendaar*. Of course, Chinta came to me whenever she found time. She blamed no one for her fate, saying, *Mu patoki*. I have sinned.

I couldn't figure out what she was talking about. She wasn't particularly interested in elucidating further. And so the days went by. I continued to watch the various scenes of life unfold in the lane where I lived as the crack on the Rays' boundary wall continued to expand. This wall was generally used for drying *ghutey*[2] in the sun. But one of the elderly, respectable gentlemen of our *para*[3] got his manservant to clear the wall, one day! That sparked off a torrent of abuse from Lakhia's mother. In spite of all this, the kathchampa tree blissfully continued to blossom round the year. Nityababu's *aunt* carefully chose some of the flowers that lay strewn on the ground for her daily Shivpuja. The futility of human behaviour apparently amused the highest branches of the tree which, basking in the golden sunlight, seemed to laugh heartily. But, of course, not everybody heard it. Meanwhile, I noticed that Chinta had put on some weight. Like the trees lining the city, she too had managed to distil some essential nourishment from the most impossible of circumstances in order to survive. She had recovered. The tattooed necklace now became her. The other day I saw her in a new sari. She told me, Ma gave me this. She had been *promoted* to 10 rupees a month.

One morning I heard a great hue and cry in our *para*. Chinta seemed to be at the centre of it all. It was a strange scene. Chinta stood there on the pavement, her head bent. And two men who had just arrived from her village were screaming at her, pointing at a 12-year-old boy who was with them. It was quite obvious that they had taken up cudgels in the name of morality and religion. One of them—fair, with a parting in the middle of his hair, chewing paan—was the most vocal. He shouted, You commit a sin and you don't want to pay the penalty! Some of the others in the crowd, who hailed from the same province as Chinta, supported him. Chinta never said a word, except, I can't afford it. What am I to do? Each time she tried to embrace the young boy, those two men would push her away.

That afternoon Chinta came to me and said, Please lend me some money. I'll pay you back.

To lend money to someone I hardly knew . . . would I get it back? But I didn't refuse at the very outset. After all, this was a good opportunity to get to hear the whole story! We've never lagged behind in curiosity, have we?

Chinta squatted near me. Tears welled up within her as she spoke. She wiped her eyes and blew her nose at intervals. Pausing to take deep breaths, she repeatedly said, I'm a great sinner. I'm cursed!

As Chinta spoke, I felt I was hearing her for the first time. She said, When I was widowed, I had just the one boy, Gopal. I had four *bighas*[4] of land, Ma. Plus two rooms, a couple of goats and a cow. But Gopal was just an infant, how could he take over the land and start farming? I pleaded with the other villagers. Some of my in-laws said, 'You're a young widow. Give us custody of your land.' I didn't agree. They turned against me. It was a terrible time, Ma. I was so young then—men began to prowl around my house after dark. I would hold on to Gopal, bar the door and call God's name. A terrible time!

She wept softly as she continued with her story. It was then that a man called Utsab went there from Calcutta. Utsab was a handsome man. He made many promises to Chinta. At first Chinta didn't encourage him at all. She locked her door against him. Then Utsab got to her through Gopal. Bought him sweets, was really kind to him. Chinta's heart began to soften. She stopped short at this point and told me, Youth is a terrible thing, Ma. The body's hunger. I became a sinner.

People were up in arms against her. Chinta was terrified. Scared of the villagers, scared for her son, scared to offer Utsab paan and *supari*—Utsab was her only support. He told her his intentions were good. He wanted to marry her. He would give her new earrings, a chain, bangles. At first, there would be a lot of talk against them. So they should leave Gopal behind for a while. Go to Calcutta. Get married there. Then return home. Without a man in the house, how would Chinta manage? Chinta told me, When he promised to marry me, I succumbed, Ma, I'm such a sinner. Then Utsab brought her to Calcutta. Chinta brought all her bell metal utensils with her, fearing that the villagers might steal them. There was nothing new about what happened next, but Chinta wasn't to know that. So she kept repeating, He ruined me and then left me. Didn't marry me, didn't give me any ornaments. He would beat me up, take all my money, and after giving me these two daughters, he absconded.

Can't you go back to the village? I asked, and she replied, I have land of my own, plenty of fish in the pond, what do I have to worry about?

Then why didn't she go back home? That was the whole problem. Chinta had to now spend 200 rupees as penance for having sinned. She had to feast the people of her village on rice and *pithey*. She also had to forsake her two girls. Only if she passed all these tests would she be accepted back by her community. Where will I get so much money, Ma? I can't afford it, so I can't go home.

The two men who had come today wielded great clout in the village. They were her late husband's uncle and his son. All this time they had looked after Chinta's son. Now it was time for the boy to be married. How much more responsibility were they expected to bear? Chinta should now get rid of the girls and go back to her village. They would organize the repentance rites and see to it that she was not ostracized. I suggested, Why don't you stay here with your son? Both of you could work and make ends meet.

Chinta shook her head. As it is she was a sinner. If she ignored what the villagers said, there would be no one to cremate her dead body. They would also make her son an outcast. How could she even think of such a dreadful fate? How to make Chinta realize that no afterlife could be bleaker than this! She kept on saying, But what am I to do with the girls? What will happen to my Giri–Gouri?

Chinta borrowed two rupees from me and left. She had to fetch some sweets, curd and *murki*[5] for her uncle-in-law. They would not eat a meal cooked by her. God helps those who have no one to turn to, said Chinta before leaving; but I couldn't fathom which god could help her now.

After eating the *murki* and sweets, the two masters of Chinta's fate came to rest on our porch. I saw her son, chewing paan, sitting down to play cards with the brahman cooks.

Problems are solved not by gods but by human beings. In the twentieth century, many things that happen around us are not in the least innocuous. And they have been happening for years. Heated discussions were held in Chinta's room. People pitched in with advice. Chinta had to borrow more money to supply them with paan and cups of tea. The paanwalla with his lewd smile was obscenely keen on getting within touching distance. The knowledge of Chinta's utter helplessness made the paan juice froth on his lips. Chinta walked carefully, bearing the curse of her youthful body. The paanwalla had money. If Chinta had been smart enough and not so scared of sinning, she could have benefited from flirting with him. Some of the rickshawallas were having great fun watching all this. Every now and then they would break into snatches of song.

The next day my maid, who had gone to the tubewell for water, brought back the news. Water splashed from the jar she was carrying as she hurried back excitedly. She said, What a sinner that woman is! She's given away her daughters! To somebody near Jagubazar. What kind of a mother is she?! *Chhi Chhi Chhi*! It seemed that the other maids and servants were feeling very righteous in the light of what Chinta had just done.

She may have given away the girls, but who had taken them? This question disturbed me every time I remembered Giri–Gauri's scrawny, stick-like forms! Who could have been so compassionate?

As I was taking my *evening walk*, our elderly neighbourhood *guardian* of public morals rushed up to me. He could barely contain himself. He said, Have you heard? What a world we live in!

I was not really interested in what could have excited this successful and enlightened gentleman. But he was dying to tell me what he knew. He said, Last night . . . well! It's rather scandalous, actually! That girl Chinta, I think you know about her . . .

He didn't wait for me to reply. He continued, Two of her so-called relatives said they had sold her little girls for 10 and eight rupees each. They wanted me to sign a paper. I drove them away. Just imagine! I'm sure you know what kind of people trade in flesh! Those pimps! It's such a big racket . . . I told them sternly, 'Whatever you've done, if you don't leave this place at once, I'm going to call the police . . .' Of course, they ran for their lives as soon as I mentioned the police!

Turning *serious*, he then said, Look at the things we have to put up with! You people are not bothered—people like you should do some *social work* in the area! So saying he trotted off to catch up with the customs officer he had just spotted. It was obvious that he was greatly excited by the whole episode.

Chinta came to say goodbye next morning. This time she was not alone. The two men flanked her, carrying her bundle. Her son too was leaving with a tin *suitcase* in hand.

She was wearing a new sari and blouse. I didn't ask where she got the money for them. I was scared. Chinta didn't cry this time. She wore the stunned, numb look of someone who has undergone some unimaginable horror. She kept looking at me with the eyes of a wounded animal. As if to gauge whether I too held her at fault.

Chinta prostrated herself before me. She said, You are a good person, Ma.

She could have left then, but she didn't. Looked out of my window with knitted eyebrows and stared aimlessly at nothing in particular. I noticed that Chinta had dark eyes and a dot tattooed on her forehead. Her eyes slowly filled with tears. She sniffled, then said, *Gariber bhagoban nai go, Ma.* There's no god for the poor.

Her companions exchanged sly glances. The younger one softened his voice and said, We'll miss the bus! I heard Chinta's son arguing with the older man, You need 10 rupees for the bus, train, snacks. Why did you buy me a three-rupee shirt?

We'll manage, he assured the boy. From those same 18 rupees, in other words.

Those who have no god have no one at all. These were Chinta's last words before she left. She crossed the road. The two men walked on either side. The boy clutched the old man's hand. He was to get married soon. The dowry he fetched would pay for the repentance rites, or this money would be added to that to help Chinta get accepted in the village. The three of them were busy discussing this while Chinta remained silent. She walked slowly, very slowly. Looked both ways before crossing the road. Almost ran to the pavement on the other side. That was the last I saw of her.

APPENDIX I

Contract Labour or Bonded Labour?

On 16 MAY, *The New Republic* of Ranchi published an account of some bonded labourers rescued from Sasaram after they had served their master for 22 years under subhuman conditions. They had been lured away to Sasaram with promises of 'good jobs', kept in captivity and made to break stones and blast rocks.

The bonded labour system was formally abolished in November 1975. Following that, a new system of recruiting bonded labourers was very quickly introduced in the bonded labour areas. Since their ex-masters would not give them work and since little was done by the state governments towards their rehabilitation, the landless ex-bonded labourers were in acute distress. Now came the agents of various masters to lure them away to faraway places with promises of good jobs. Once they reached these places, they found themselves in a worse form of bondage.

The young ones are waiting for the inevitable *dalal*[1] to come one day and take them away. Many are going. They hear of their good fortune in the weekly *haat*. The masters are good, give two square meals a day. Even the young ones are not against becoming a *kamia* or a *seokia*. 'What to do? There is nothing else for the likes of us.' The land given to the freed bonded labourers is uncultivable. The good land is held by the master, though the ownership-paper is in the freed labourer's name. There is no water for drinking or irrigation; no chance of being employed by government agencies for road-repairing, timber-felling, etc. Though Palamau is a labour-surplus and poverty-stricken district, outside labour is brought in for such work. Forsaken by the government and society, these people, in order to stay alive, enter debt-bondage. They do not have any alternative.

I stared at the face of the young boy. What would he become? A *seokia*, a *kamia*, a *jonwar*? A *harwaha*, a *charwaha*?[2] Would he receive some *tanr*, dry *palhatu*[3] land? *Palhatu* land is not given away to the cattlegrazer or *charwaha*, who just cultivates it as long as he is in service. I have spelt out the background in some detail in order to stress the conditions in which poor adivasis, Muslims and scheduled caste people are recruited by the labour-contractors.

Some of my friends in the villages and forests are very unusual, but Purnendu Mazoomdar is in a class by himself. I am sure that there are very few like him anywhere. His is a household name in the poor villages of Tamar, Bundu, Torpa, Khunti, Chakradharpur, Monoharpur, Gua—over a wide region covering the 2 districts of Ranchi and Singbhum. He is with the poor tribals and non-tribals in their struggle to gain their forest rights, in their fight with the factory and mine owners against prolonged lockouts, in their battle to cling to the land others snatch away from them. Short, animated and simple, this middle-aged man speaks many tribal languages and is considered the tribal's true friend. He starves with the tribals, stays with them, and walks hundreds of miles to visit his people when they are in distress. He is also the general secretary of the Mineral Workers' Union, Chakradharpur.

A few months ago he came to me with Laru Jonko, a remarkable Ho woman. She was the president of the Mahila Samiti of Chiriburu and had just succeeded in tracing several adivasi girls who were missing from the interior villages of Singbhum. These girls were working in brick kilns around Calcutta. The story was revealing.

The brick-kiln owners of West Bengal are mostly from north Bihar. This practice of recruitment of adivasi labour must be quite old. Adivasi women, ex-concubines of the kiln owners, are sent to remote villages. The link railway stations are Chaibasa, Sonwa, Pendrasali and Chakradharpur. These recruiting women are called *sardars*. They go to the village *haats* and lure young girls with tales of good jobs near the magic city of Calcutta.

Chiriburu is the place where the Orissa Cement Company has a quartzite mine. This mine has been under illegal lockout by the owners since 8 March 1979 and 2000 adivasi *rejas* have been starving as a result. Gua leaped into the limelight in 1980. This is the region where militant and indomitable tribals and non-tribals are fighting for their rights to the forest and the land. Relentless police and military repression goes on here. After the Gua firing, ploughs have been broken, cattle and poultry seized, foodgrains destroyed; women have lost *izzat* and huts have been razed to the ground. Women can survive on jungle roots and fruits but they need money to buy clothes. So it has been easy for the *sardars* to collect a willing batch of girls, bribe the police, railway police and the political parties, and bring the girls to Calcutta.

Each kiln employs 200 to 400 *rejas*, and each *sardar* receives Rs 30–40 commission for each *reja*, so it is easy to understand that the lure of ready money is too much for the *sardar*. Why does the *sardar* do it, being a tribal herself? I have said that the *sardars* are one-time concubines of the kiln owners, and close association with the owners corrupts these women. They are usually despised by their own folk. They become virtual outcasts.

I find, from the account of Purnendu Mazoomdar, that the women *sardars*, Sona Jonko and Nandi Jamuda, have supplied 34 *rejas* to the kilns of Magra in West Bengal from the villages of Komay, Ichakuti and Banka, all under Chakradharpur police station. Two male *sardars*, Dibru Lohar and Madru Angari, have supplied, to the same kiln, 5 girls from the villages of Sagipi, Shengao and Otuoti under the same police station.

The kiln owners or *bhatta-maliks* begin by buying paddy land from poor peasants to build the kiln. Since the adjoining paddy fields are ruined by constant use by the *rejas* as passage to the *bhatta*, the owners ultimately sell them to the *bhatta-malik*. The *rejas* receive 1 token or *tikli* for carrying 10 unbaked bricks over 300 to 400 yards. The same payment is received for carrying 10 baked or *pucca* bricks. For unbaked bricks, 20 tokens mean Re 1. One rupee for carrying 200 *kutcha* bricks. For *pucca* bricks, 44 tokens mean Re 1. One rupee for carrying 440 *pucca* bricks. The *rejas* cannot earn more than Rs 4–5 per day. Children aged 10–12 constitute 25 per cent of the total labour strength. Where an adult *reja* earns Rs 25–30 a week, a child earns Rs 10–15. However, an adult actually receives only Rs 15 per week and a child Rs 10. An adult can buy 4 kilos of rice per week and a child 3 kilos. Rice with salt is their only food. Do they get the rest of their wages when they go home? No, never. Paupers they come and paupers they go. Yet they come again the next year. Why?

Sardars who have become too recognized do not approach the prospective *rejas* directly, but send sub-agents. They explore fresh areas. The *rejas* who have had a bad experience are easily misled when a new agent approaches them and promises better working conditions. The last and ultimate decider of their fate, of course, is the state government's total apathy towards them. 1980 was a drought year, so there was remission of land tax. This year, tax arrears are being collected with much *zulm*.[4] Cause enough to drive these people to desperate measures. We are talking of a region where Rs 30 a month is considered a handsome income for an adult and an income of Rs 20 per month is nearer reality. The villagers have land, but it is unproductive and dry. Villagers living in the neighbourhood of a town can sell firewood in the town market. Those living in the remote interior cannot. So they go to the *sardars*. The *sardars* prefer young, unmarried girls. They are better workers and good for sale.

They force these young girls to sleep with the owners, the supervising staff, the truck drivers, *khalasis*[5] and local *mastaans*. Anyone who refuses to cooperate is first locked up in a room, beaten and then seared with a hot iron. It is usual to make a girl drink heavily and then send her for the master's pleasure. A young Ho girl, aged 16, has been compelled to become the *aurat* of an aged kiln owner at Gajipara in 24 Parganas, West Bengal. She is from the village Dharamsai under Chakradharpur police station.

In politically conscious West Bengal these *rejas* are denied a minimum wage, medical facilities, maternity leave or any kind of leave, and, of course, the right to form a union. There is no attendance or pay register, identity card or employment card. The set-up is very cruel and very cunning. It is impossible for an outsider to break into the fortress of the *bhattas*. The *rejas* cannot leave the *bhatta* or talk to anyone without the prior permission of the owner. The *sardar* never lets them out of her sight. A close guard is kept on them.

These unfortunate beings live in *jhopris* worse than pig holes. There are no sanitary arrangements, nor any drinking water where they work through the summer days. The kiln is closed with the onset of the monsoons and the *rejas* are sent home.

Male recruiting *sardar* Ponka Gagrai of village Dhipasai, Chakradharpur police station, avoids entering village Bari for fear of a possible encounter with Budhu Oihar and Kanklo Gop. He had taken away Budhu's daughter Pechi and Kanklo's daughter Jema 6 years ago to Patna and the two girls have not come back ever since. From Kharswan and Sagipi villages he supplied 100 labourers to Bakhtiarpur for a farm owner. In November 1980 he took to Benares seven girls from Sagipi. From Kharswan he supplied Shilai Bodra and 34 more girls to a kiln owner of Ayodhya. Kachi Daroga, P. O. Jatla, Patna, received 30 to 35 girls. All these girls are young and many of them physically attractive. Not all of them will come back after the brick-making season is over. A mother sings to the baby on her lap:

My Bali could live on forest fruits,
My Bali could live on jungle roots;

But trees, alas, do not saris grow,
So to the *bhatta* my Bali had to go.
My Bali had to go.

Where are the Jagtas and Balis and Charibas? If you ask the parents, they say simply that life was too hard, survival was threatened, the *bhattas* called out to them and they left.

I have spoken of West Bengal. What happens in Bihar? Bihar, to me, is the true mirror of India. Bihar has everything in plenty. Even bonded and contract labourers.

The Oraon, Ho and Munda tribals meet the needs of hundreds of kilns on the Ganges, at Muzaffarpur, Samastipur, Bhojpur, Begusarai, Monghyr, Purnea, Gaya, Patna and Chhapra. The coolie *jhopris* are within the towns and cities, yet the tribals stay imprisoned there, closely guarded by the musclemen of the owners. Theirs is a medieval existence far beyond the reach of statutory labour law benefits and democratic rights.

The recruiting end is in the hands of the *sardars*. They take the *munshis* of the owner to their villages and keep them carefully concealed. August and September, the monsoon months, are the worst for the tribals. This is the time when they are starving, totally helpless. The *munshi* and the *sardar* arrange grand feasts and invite the local youth. Through them they get to know of the whereabouts of girls. Then they make the rounds with ready cash in hand. The *munshi* pays *dadan* or advance money to the parents of the girls. Once the parents accept Rs 100–150 from the *munshi*, the girls become contract-bound. They cannot refuse to go and work. In the *bhatta*, life undergoes a change: 12–14 hours of work a day, loading and unloading bricks, compulsory sex with the owner or his men in the early hours of the night, sleep in the *jhopri* in the late hours. No medical or sanitary arrangements.

A *reja* may have earned Rs 30–35 in a week, but receives only Rs 15 as *khoraki*.[6] The rest she never gets. When the kiln closes down, the *reja* is given a sari and a railway ticket. The rest, she is told, has been adjusted against her *khoraki* and the *dadan* her parents received.

None of these facts can be verified easily as there is no wage or attendance register, no employment card. Women in the late stages of pregnancy work, because there is no maternity leave. Their lot is worse than that of those in the unorganized sector. A beggar can go abegging where he chooses. A contract-labourer cannot. He does not have any freedom.

What drives them to the brick kilns? Poverty does. Poverty and the deep-rooted apathy of the state government towards adopting any remedial measures to remove the root causes of chronic poverty. Singbhum and Ranchi. The cradles of the Kol, Tamar, Birsa, Jharkhand and other movements. By the Bihar Government's own admission, Chhotanagpur has only 2 per cent land area under irrigation and 5 per cent under electrification. Only the industries and the towns receive electricity. There is no arrangement for irrigation through electricity. Lift irrigation is for show and publicity, not for the cultivator. The Chaibasa project is supposed to be under operation, but thousands of villages do not have even a well for drinking water. Under Gua police station, the tribals drink water from the Koina river which is polluted by the Khiriburu washery plant. The Munda-dominated Khunti subdivision has had no project for irrigation.

The Bihar Government collects, on each rupee paid towards land rent, 40 paise as cess for health, 40 paise as cess for education and 20 paise as cess for roads. Sounds very nice and reads better on paper. But how is this money spent in the region from where the contract-bound labourers come? Banka, under Chaibasa police station, has no school building, though there is a teacher. Guigaon under Chakradharpur police station has a school building. Dalbhanga is a predominantly Munda region and is now under Kuchai police station within Seraikela subdivision. It belonged to Tamar police station till 1954. Then came the Boundary Commission and, in order to have Oriya-majority Seraikela within Singbhum, Bihar, 30 *moujas*[7] from the predominantly Mundari language area under Tamar police station were added to Seraikela. Seraikela became a part of Singbhum. But the Mundas of this region are not at all happy over the surgical operation on the regional map. They have to keep close connections with the Mundari area for social purposes and they feel cut off. In 1968 the government took over a high school at Dalbhanga and a hostel for the tribal students. Both were built with mud. The Bihar Government has not found time to convert these into *pucca* buildings in 13 years, nor funds to repair them. These are only a few of the innumerable instances of governmental apathy towards the tribal regions. There are lakhs and lakhs of tribals in Singbhum and Ranchi. A majority of them pay land rent. What does the almighty *sarkar* do with the 40 paise cess per rupee of land rent they pay for education?

For the poor tribal, money is blood. Land is *tanr, banjhara*. Each rupee is earned by selling so many bundles of firewood, so many baskets of *chiranji*, by breaking so many stones, by working so many hours in the mines. Even after the sanction of a primary school for every 100 homesteads, the people remain illiterate. In many schools the teachers don't attend work. They have their own business or trade or shop to look after. The *pradhan* of Sagipi Primary School carries on a brisk business buying *mowa*, goats, silkworm, etc., from the villagers and selling them to traders. This worthy was once *gheraoed*. Complaints against him were submitted to the proper authority, but to no avail. Teachers from north Bihar posted in the tribal region have been caught lending money, buying land or taking *bandobasti*[8] land. Stipends for scheduled caste and tribal boys in primary schools are a great blessing to the teachers who take a nice 'cut' from the money which is sent in lump sums. A Mundari song runs like this:

Rando, Rando, come to school!
Mata, Mata, where are you?
Rando and Mata and the other boys
Graze the cow, tend the goat.
The *Masterji* sits in his shop.

The tribals pay 40 paise for health and medical care and what do they get in return? Lotapahar has a primary health unit but no doctor. So the unit is useless. Dulmi has a doctor but the health unit building is only half-built. Kukru has a dispensary attended by a compounder but no medicine and no doctor. Chhotonagra under Gua police station has no doctor but there is a dispensary. Situated in the deep interior, Chhotonagra did not have any Sahus till 1962. Now there are 4 Sahus who act as moneylenders, land-usurpers and police agents. The poor of the area are malaria-ridden. Women die at childbirth. Infant and child mortality is high.

The lack of doctors and medicine causes death. And when death, disease or epidemic frequents the lonely villages, the villagers launch a witch-hunt, identify someone as a witch and kill her. In Sagipi village in 1978 child mortality was high. The villagers were sure that a witch was causing these deaths. An old Christian tribal woman was identified as the witch. She was a person of some means, had a husband, grown-up sons, grandchildren. The villagers invited her for a *diang* (rice liquor) drinking session and killed her. In January 1981, at Dhangaon under Chakradharpur police station, a Ho woman aged 54 was killed in broad daylight. After a week her widowed daughter was also killed at night, while she was sleeping with her children in their hut. Reason? Some 4 or 5 people were suffering from the same sort of sore on their right legs. The witch must have caused those sores.

Chiriburu Mahila Samaj, under the leadership of the courageous Ho woman, Laru Jonko, has launched a mass signature campaign against witch-hunting. Their cry is, 'Medical facilities are needed. This witch-hunting is barbarous and wrong. Doctors and medicine will bring succour to the people. We achieve nothing by killing innocent women.'

Till now almost Rs 3,000 crores have been spent on 'tribal development' in Chhotanagpur. The Sixth Plan has allotted Rs 800 crore. But even after 5 Plans nothing has reached the area. The people have been left in primeval darkness. Officially, the leasing of forests to contractors has been abolished. The declaration has been given much publicity. The announcement came after the Gua firing. But contractors are felling trees in the Jaraikela forest under Sarenda division, all right. The forests in the Ranka *mouja* under Chandil police station are serving their death sentence. Mango, *jamun*, *pial*, *kendu*, *bael*, all fruit-bearing trees, are exempt from felling under the Forest Acts. But the contractor's axe is felling them, too. The tribals and poor villagers are, naturally, desperate. After the Gua firing, the government declared that there would be no collection from the weekly *haats*. The *haat masul* was abolished. Yet *haat masul* is definitely exacted in one of the biggest *haats* of Singbhum district, the Kukru *haat* under Ichagarh police station. Previously, the *masul* was shared equally by the tribal buyer and the north Bihari seller. Now the purchaser of a cow or vegetables or paddy or clothes has to pay the full amount. In the dry months *haat masul* from Kukru is Rs 2,000 per week. In winter it is Rs 4,000. The Raja of Ichagarh is the recipient of this *masul* which is said to be collected for the development of Ichagarh High School. It is hard to understand why this school has not been taken over by the government. It is certain that the money does nothing for the school. Students pay their fees. The school goes on. The landless Jhora people have been running the ferry boats on the Koel, Koina and Subarnarekha for ages. Now the Bihar Government has leased out the ferries to contractors. The Jhoras are unemployed. At places the village panchayat has been handling the contracts.

What happens to the *kendu* or *bidi* leaves? Previously the poor villagers grew *kendu* trees on their land and sold the leaves to the traders. January to March is the plucking season. A family could earn Rs 400–500 per season. The Bihar Government leased out the plucking right to contractors; now the villagers are the contractors' labourers. For 100 *kendu* leaves (about a kg) he receives Rs 1.75 when he plucks in a government forest. And in the open market the rate is Rs 10 per kg. The contractors' rate is Re 1 for 100 *keris* or bundles. One *keri* contains 25 leaves. To pluck 2,500 leaves a man or a woman works from 4 in the morning till 4 in the afternoon in the depths of the forest, and receives Re 1. The contractor will sell that quantity for Rs 250. I cite these figures to show the pattern of exploitation.

The Mahalis, like the Jhoras, have been reduced to destitution. They are traditionally basket-weavers. Previously they collected bamboo from the forests. Then came forest laws. They had to obtain permission from the Forest Department and pay *masul* for bamboo, the raw material for baskets and winnows. The ruthless deforestation by the contractors has caused them great suffering.

Tales of woe and exploitation on the one hand; the pulse of resistance mounting on the other. The Jharkhand demand is set against such a background. When these people take to violence, they do it out of sheer desperation.

I started with contract-labourers and shall conclude my account with them. Not only women, men, too, are helpless. I cite 2 cases.

▸ 1. Amar Ekka, a Christian Munda and the son of Albis Ekka, was 19 years old in 1976. The family had 8 members, 10 to 12 acres of land with a yield of 30 maunds. Amar was educated upto class 8. Fagu Sahu recruited him in 1976. Amar says, 'I went to Hurda Basar and this agent said that he would take us to Punjab and get us good jobs. I went to Bano, from there to Tati, from Tati to Batia, from Batia to Gomoh. At Gomoh I got into the Amritsar Mail. We got down at Tanda Hurmur station. Then we went along with Mahendra Singh who was the coolie agent for Punjab. Fagu Sahu sold us to Mahendra. We were 5 or 6 boys. We stayed for 8 days at Pathankot. The farmer Makhan Singh promised to pay Rs 60 per month as wages plus food, clothes, etc. From 4 a.m. I looked after cattle till 8 a.m. From 8 a.m. I watered the wheat fields. I was ill-treated, beaten and harassed by Makhan Singh and his family members. My wage was raised to Rs 80. After 6 months I wanted to leave. Makhan did not give me 2 months' wages. He said he had paid me and was adjusting the money. I ran away from his place one day at 3 a.m. By train I reached Tanda Hurmur. There Darshan Singh, a teacher, employed me at Rs 100 per month. He had 2,000 cows and buffaloes and milking was operated electrically. I worked till 1979 and my wage was Rs 175 per month. Then I left.'

▸ 2. Sura Pai, a Raotia boy from Buruichanda was brought to Ferozepur by Shivshankar Sahu and sold to Diwan Singh of Sandwala for Rs 250. 'Diwan Singh told me, "I have purchased you, so I won't give you anything for 2 months. After 2 months, I will pay you Rs 100 a month with food." I worked there for 4 months and was inhumanly treated. The local agricultural labourers asked me, "Why do you work for so little? We work for Rs 10/12 a day." I ran away after 4 months when my owner refused to pay me anything. I sold some wheat for Rs 8 and went by train to Ludhiana. There I met Barna Karkota of Harta village who was sold to Surjeet Singh, Diwan Singh's brother and a *sarpanch*.[9] Barna was running away from his owner, a very cruel man. At Ludhiana we worked at Jagdamba Wool Mill at Rs 170 per month and 4 hours' overtime benefit. After 2 months I got Rs 180 per month. I spent Rs 100 on food and lodging. After I saved some money I returned home.'

We know some of these details from Purnendu Mazoomdar's untiring efforts to uncover the pattern of exploitation in Singbhum and Ranchi. The Bihar Government realizes Rs 30 crore from the forests of Chhotanagpur and Rs 10 crore from the Excise Department. The royalty received from the mines and industries must be fabulous. If forest revenue received by the government is Rs 30 crore, what must the contractors be earning? Their palaces in Ranchi and north Bihar give some idea. As long as Chhotanagpur is kept for exploitation alone, agents and *sardars* will go on haunting the destitute villages. Men and women will migrate to faraway places. Some will come back, some will not. Punjab and Haryana will have slaves. West Bengal and the rest of Bihar, *bhatta-coolies*. Kiln owners, *mastaans* and truck drivers will have their pot of flesh and all will be happy except the tribals and the non-tribal poor. But they are expendable.

Economic and Political Weekly, *6 June 1981.*
Reprinted in Dust on the Road: The Activist Writings of Mahasweta Devi (*Calcutta*: *Seagull Books*, *1997*)

APPENDIX II

Birbhum Punjab

THE BENGALI READER IS rarely informed about the oppression and extortion of migrant labourers who change hands through various contractors and middlemen.

In Ranchi, for example, there are many workers from Punjab in Bharat Heavy Engineering Limited and other similar establishments. These men serve as local contacts for big farmers and brick kiln owners of Punjab. In turn, they contact those who have an easy and frequent access to the villages. The village middlemen arrange for the supply of slave labourers. The owners pay between Rs 200–300 per labourer to the agents and between Rs 100–150 to the middlemen in the villages. Both Ranchi and Singbhum are impoverished areas. It's quite strange, is it not? Both these places, especially Singbhum, are very rich in mineral and forest resources. Singbhum ensures that millions of rupees flow into the coffers of the Tatas, the Birlas and the Dalmiyas. And people from both these places throng to board the Tata–Amritsar Mail, tempted by nothing more than the hope of a decent meal a day. Their destinations are varied—places like Tandawala, Raipura, Jallandhar,

Amritsar, Ludhiana. The middleman, having bribed the railway police and the ticket collector, does not have to bother about buying tickets for them.

On arriving in Punjab, they are harassed—often beaten up—by the ticket collector and the GRP for travelling without tickets, and are forced to relinquish whatever money they have on them. Then they are handed over to the Punjabi owners. This is how coolies are illegally exchanged between Bihar and Punjab. And all these people, from the department of railways to the local agents to the middlemen in the villages, have a stake in this trade.

Why do the owners insist on paying these middlemen money and keeping them happy?

We shall soon see why . . .

▸ 1. Constable Rautia. Son of Dulu Rautia. Village and Post Office Raikera. Thana Bano. District Ranchi. The village middleman Shibshankar Shahu sold the constable for Rs 300 to Narana Singh of Faridkot district. A year later, the constable's wife Birsi, back in the village of Raikera, received a letter. She learnt that the constable was being subjected to daily beatings and starvation. Ignorant of the way back to Ranchi, he was unable to return home. Another letter followed, written by an observer sympathetic to the constable's condition. That letter said that the constable was made to work 16–18 hours every day. All his attempts to escape had met with beatings so severe that each time he was reduced to a bloodied mass. Nevertheless, he managed to escape, and hid in the sugarcane fields where Narana's men found him three days later. Dragging him back to the owner's house, they tortured him by simultaneously beating him and branding him with a piece of hot iron. Due to which, he finally died on 10 May 1981.

Narana Singh wrote an undated letter informing the family that the constable was dead. And that he was sending Birsi Rs 500 as salary owed to his employee.

▸ 2. Loknath Harijan (25), his wife Sombari (20) and their child from the village of Jorobori, District Ranchi, Bano Thana, were sold to Karnal Singh of Johnara Basti village of Punjab by the village middleman Demo Chik. Karnal Singh promised to pay Rs 100 and Rs 30 to Loknath and Sombari respectively, every month. And to provide for their meals. Loknath used to work in the cattle sheds from four to eight in the morning. And then, till eight at night, he would work in the fields, farming wheat. Sombari used to start work at four in the morning, sweeping and swabbing the cattle shed and the house, washing utensils, washing clothes, and then work in the sugarcane fields. Sombari was also raped by Karnal, every day. And was forced to undergo an abortion when she conceived. Loknath and Sombari left this job after nine months. At the time, instead of the Rs 1,170 which they had earned over this period, they were paid only Rs 500.

▸ 3. Phagu Shahu, a middleman from Harani village, Bano Thana, sold Gurumohan Rautia (28), his wife Ratni (22), and their three children to Sardar Niranjan Singh of Haripur village, in the Firozepur district of Punjab, for Rs 400. Niranjan owned an electric pump, a washing machine and a tractor. Guru was promised Rs 80 per month and Ratni, Rs 40. Just as in the instance cited above, this couple too worked for 16–18 hours every day. Ratni and her children would work in the sugarcane fields. There, in the small hut in the middle, supposedly meant for keeping a watch over the crops, Niranjan and his male relatives and friends used to rape Ratni every day, even as her children looked on. Within four months Ratni was forced to undergo an abortion. Assisted by the local farm workers, under cover of night, Guru and Ratni managed to escape. Till then, they had not received a single rupee by way of pay. After this, they sought employment under Karnal Singh of Johaner Basti. Here too, they worked for the same 16–18 hour stretch and Ratni continued to be raped, this time by Karnal. But where could they run to, with their three children? Guru and Ratni had no choice but to endure every hardship. After a month, they ran away. To Sardar Preetam Singh, in Kosa village. Once again, they worked for 16–18 hours every day and Guru's wife was raped continually. After 12 days, they sought work at Hoshiarpur, from Sardar Gyan Singh. And remained in his employment for four months and were exploited in an identical manner. Ratni continued to be raped. Then they moved to Badala village, in Kapurtala and began to work for Sardar Sarban Singh. He too made them work mercilessly, although he never laid a finger on Ratni, and provided the entire family with plenty to eat. A month later, one of Sarban's relatives, a young Sardar, raped Ratni. Collecting 150 rupees from Sarban, Guru and Ratni left for home.

▸ 4. Ramesh Rautia was sold by Demo Chik for Rs 300 to Sardar Raghubir Singh of Pike Basti village, in the district of Firozepur. He was to work for a monthly salary of Rs 30. Ramesh was supposed to take his owner's children to school and bring them back home, go door to door selling milk and collecting payment, cutting straw to feed the household cattle, taking food for the farmers working in the fields, and so on. He was regularly abused sexually by the men in the family. Two years later, Ramesh returned home having received only Rs 300.

▸ 5. Shibshankar Shahu, mentioned earlier, sold Mishu Rautia for Rs 300 to Banta Singh, of Kejur Basti village, in the district of Firozepur. After a fortnight, Banta Singh sold Rautia for Rs 500 to Makhan Singh of Parak Basti village. When Mishu finally returned home, of the Rs 840 he had earned by way of salary, he had been paid only Rs 600.

▸ 6. Chhoto Rautia—the man sold by Shibshankar Shahu—has said, 'Shibshankar took us, a group of 20 youngsters, aged about 16–18, to Banta Singh of Kejur Basti, who then bought us at a wholesale rate. For each one of us, Shibshankar got between Rs 200–300. We worked on the wheat fields for 16–18 hours every day, for 10 days, living on just 10 dried chapatis. Then I was sold to Sardar Jata Singh of Parak Basti village for Rs 350. My salary was fixed at Rs 100 per month. I worked 16–18 hours, every day, for eight months and wasn't paid a single rupee. And I was beaten, starved and tortured daily. I ran away from there and went to Preetam Singh in the village of Saptewala, in Firozepur. My salary was fixed at Rs 100. I was beaten daily by the members of the household, old or young. At night, they used to keep me locked up like an animal. After three months, I received Rs 150. And then I fled. I met up with another coolie, and the two of us somehow managed to come back home.'

Now, let me tell you that—

The fact that these bonded labourers received Rs 100, 150, 300 means that they were not provided with either a railway ticket or the fare for a train ticket or clothes.

The table below will indicate why the landowners of Punjab prefer to use slave labour despite the availability of local farmhands. And how they make a profit irrespective of the amount of money they pay to the village middlemen and to the local agents (in Ranchi).

Wages prevalent in 1980, in Ludhiana—

Labour costs per acre:

wheat farming	Rs 75
sowing paddy	Rs 115
harvesting and threshing paddy	Rs 164

Percentage of slave labour entering

	all of Punjab	Ludhiana
1972	45%	5.26%
1980	34.7%	40.59%

For harvesting—the minimum wage for a local Punjabi farmhand is Rs 17.55; the farmhand is actually paid Rs 10.60; each slave labourer is paid Rs 10.08.

The funny thing is that, if a Punjabi farmhand is hired, he will be paid according to the above rates, whereas slave labourers are paid nothing. In their case, the above rates remain merely numbers on paper.

What is worth noticing is that the local farmhands are actually quite sympathetic towards these coolies. Even though they find it difficult to find employment, they help these slave labourers to escape their harsh conditions. In the brick kilns of West Bengal too, the local labourers are sympathetic to the condition of those purchased from other states. The Punjabi landowners are enraged at this particular attitude of the local labourers.

The big farmers of Punjab are quite wealthy and travel abroad frequently. The farmhands of Punjab work for exactly 8 hours a day and demand a higher rate of wages. The bonded labourers work for 16 hours just to fend off starvation. The state and central government subsidize costs for these big farmers because they are apparently responsible for agricultural growth. If these farmers can employ the country's bonded labourers, their profits increase.

Every grain of wheat from Punjab being sold in the ration shops [under our public distribution system] is stained with the blood of these slave labourers. The Punjabi farmer is lauded in newspapers and films, at home and abroad. Punjab is synonymous with a thriving hotel industry, lots of sports, the armed forces, and successful contractors and businessmen.

The agricultural prosperity of Punjab has been achieved at the cost of the lives of these slave labourers. Why do these coolies go to Punjab? Because back home, starvation stares them in the face.

The areas from which these slave labourers come are poverty stricken to a terrifying degree. I shall speak of that at some other time.

Dainik Basumati, *2 December 1981.*

Translated by Sunandini Banerjee.

Notes

'Dhouli'

1 Literally, 'one who is fair.'

2 'Devta' or god/master.

3 Small oil lamp.

4 A raised platform.

5 Low-caste untouchables.

6 A *dusad* neighbourhood.

7 Mother, generally used as a form of address for a goddess or holy woman.

8 Ironically, used for both a widow and a prostitute.

9 A sweetmeat made from sesame.

10 The ceremony to mark a girl's attaining puberty, when she is sent to live with her husband.

11 Small brass pot for carrying water.

12 Like the koel or cuckoo.

13 Gramflour; a cheap but nourishing staple usually eaten by the very poor.

14 Maize.

15 A dagger-like weapon.

16 Literally, 'Well done!'

17 Subjects.

'Shanichari'

1 A sweetmeat usually with coconut stuffing.

2 Traditional tribal youth commune for boys.

3 Traditional tribal youth commune for girls.

4 A district defined for tax collection purposes.

5 Literally, a cobra.

6 Woman labourer in a brick kiln.

7 Lesser foodgrains.

8 Type of lentil.

9 Deep-fried disc of flour, a treat associated with celebrations and the good life.

10 Shiny, new, glossy, gleaming.

11 Flaunting, brazen.

12 Literally, 'There! His/Her memory has come, but He/She has not.'

13 Independence, for the second time; in this context, economic independence.

14 An end to oppression.

15 A proverbial expression literally meaning, 'Delhi is a long way off,' and implying that the task at hand is a long way from completion.

16 The Central Reserve Police Force and the Border Security Force.

17 Saratchandra Chattopadhyay's famous Bengali novel, well-known to the Bengali middle-class readership.

18 General Railway Police.

19 Literally, abode of Indra. Indra, the King of Gods, lived in Indrapuri, famed for its magnificent architecture.

20 Police Station.

21 Secretary.

22 Token.

23 A simple meal of handmade wheatbread and vegetables.

24 Term used by the tribals for non-tribal intruders.

25 A very cheap sari distributed through ration shops.

26 A tribal custom whereby if a child's father or mother happens to be a non-tribal, he/she has to get married to a person of similar parentage.

'The Fairytale of Rajabasha'

1 Drum.

2 Type of lentil.

3 The naming ceremony of the Ho tribe. Some rice is floated in a basin of water and the child is called by different names. A good response from the child decides the name.

4 Land of the Kol tribe. Ho, Kol, Munda, Oraon and Santhals mainly live in Kolhan which is the Singbhum district of Jharkhand.

5 Hos are generally buried. Till the 1980s, each family used to have a burial ground of its own.

6 Ho, Mundari, Kol and Santali word for the sal tree.

7 A watery gruel.

8 Bhaadro marks the beginning of the Autumn season. Bhaadro spans from mid-August to mid-September.

9 A flexible word used to mean goods, stuff or material.

10 Type of edible fruit.

11 A measure of weight, little less than a kilo.

12 A maund is equivalent to 40 kilos.

13 Wild, not educated.

14 Literally, 'a Punjabi farmer is the ideal farmer;' a saying made popular with the Green Revolution in India.

15 Refers to the Jharkhand movement. The author did not use the word 'Jharkhand' because the story was

written in the early 1980s when the tribal movement for a separate state had reached its peak. At present, India has a separate state called Jharkhand.

16 One-twentieth of a bigha.

17 Wild animals.

18 The land of the brave, the land of heroes.

19 Basket-weavers.

'Chinta'

1 Betel nut.

2 Cowdung cakes.

3 Neighbourhood.

4 Measure of land equal to one-third of an acre.

5 A sweetmeat made of parched rice.

Appendix I: Contract Labour or Bonded Labour?

1 Middleman.

2 *Seokia*, *kamia*, *jonwar*, *harwaha* and *charwaha* are different types of bonded labourers.

3 Land given to the *harwaha* strictly for the duration of the bonded period.

4 Oppression.

5 Helpers.

6 Daily meal.

7 A group of villages treated as an administrative unit for collection of land revenues.

8 A land settlement measure through which land is distributed to the landless.

9 Head of the panchayat.